The Originals

a novel by

L.E. Vollick

© L.E. Vollick, 2002
First Edition

New Writers Series edited by Robert Allen

Design by conundrum
Author photos by Jill Goldberg

An excerpt from this novel appeared in *Matrix #60*

National Library of Canada Cataloguing in Publication Data

Vollick, L. E. (Lindsay Erin), 1973-
    The originals

ISBN 0-919688-49-7 (bound), — ISBN 0-919688-47-0 (pbk.)

    I. Title.

PS8593.O45O75 2002   C813'.6   C2002-900655-4
PR9199.4.V64O75 2002

DC BOOKS / LIVRES DC

Box 662, 950 Decarie, Montreal, Quebec
H4L 4V9, Canada

Contents

Québec ⬚⬚

The Canada Council | Le Conseil des Arts
for the Arts | du Canada

DC Books gratefully acknowledges the support of The Canada
Council for the Arts and of SODEC for our publishing program.

for **Matt Cohen**—
smiling down from writer's heaven
for your faith.

"As once as far as Angels ken he views
The dismal Situation waste and wild."

—John Milton, *Book I, Paradise Lost*

"He was safe here; this was the place he loved—
sanctuary, the paradise of his despair."

—Malcolm Lowry, *Under the Volcano*

"We have a different regard for
human life than those monsters do."

**—U.S. President Ronald Reagan
on the Soviets, 1980**

"Every gun that is made, every warship launched, every
rocket fired signifies, in the final sense, a theft from those
who hunger and are not fed, those who are cold and are not
clothed. This world in arms is not spending money alone.
It is spending the sweat of its laborers, the genius of its
scientists, the hopes of its children.... Under the cloud of
threatening war, it is humanity hanging from a cross of iron."

—U.S. President Dwight Eisenhower

Dear Mr. Andropov,

My name is Samantha Smith. I am ten years old. Congratulations on your new job. I have been worrying about Russia and the United States getting into a nuclear war. Are you going to vote to have a war or not? If you aren't please tell me how you are going to help to not have a war. This question you do not have to answer, but I would like to know why you want to conquer the world or at least our country. God made the world for us to live together in peace and not to fight.

Sincerely,
Samantha Smith

Modern Women

We aren't original, PK says, so how come we feel so alone? I ponder this as we shuffle through Olivia Newton John and Skinny Puppy records, play them on his Walt Disney record player that he found in the trash. He takes another cigarette from our short stubby pack, leans his back against the wall on his vermin-infested mattress. This is the hole that he calls 'Livin' Easy', although it isn't—atop Sing's Convenience, with its broad, striped green and white awning and wooden blocks piled high with fruit and flowers. There's nothing convenient about PK's sink filled with butts and rusting Spaghetti-o's cans. Or the hot plate perched on his makeshift counter and the tiny gash of a closet smeared with clothes. And even his lamp—the naked woman arching upwards with breasts like oxygen masks—is not exactly wholesome. But we aren't really alone. Everyone we know lives the same way.

When I was ten there was this older guy who hopped around talking to the older girls who had, to say the least, a little more on top than me. He *hopped* because he had this full-length, hot as hell leg cast and when he wanted to get places more quickly than Sweeney (the garbage picking old-timer who lived in a cardboard box beside our tenement, and in the foyer during the coldest months) he had to hop.

Me, I was this skinny little thing, the kind who wasn't going to develop anything even if you drew them on. I wore nothing but my brothers' hand-me-down soccer t's, cut-off shorts, Oilers and Leafs jerseys, Harley t's, my brothers' jeans with holes in each extravagantly ripped knee. So of course I didn't understand it when he paid so much attention to me, called me his little sweetheart, his little girlfriend. I didn't understand it when he would say, out of the hearing range of my brothers, "Hey sweetiepie, when you gonna grow up and be my girl?" I liked his eyes. Dave had these chocolate-brown eyes that never blinked when he was looking at someone. And Dave sure loved to look, smiling away at me as if we were on one of those stupid soap operas.

He hung around but I never did find out where he lived. Then there was this day Dave came around wearing a pair of jeans that didn't have one of the legs cut off.

"Hi sweetie," he said to me. A handful of girls were playing double dutch, and I was watching on the sidelines. On the front steps of the building a bunch of the guys were smoking doobs and watching the girls jiggle. Dave grinned and waved his cane at them.

"Did ya get your cast off?" I asked him.

"Yeah. C'mere and give me a hug," he said. I did, and he squeezed me so hard I couldn't breathe for a minute.

"Show me," I said, and he rolled up the cuff. I could see from the corner of my eye everyone was trying to catch a glimpse of it, and when the jean came up far enough I could see why. All the skin was this prickly goose skin. It was just like the skin of a supermarket chicken, loose and pasty. "Can I touch it?"

"Yup. But go easy, eh?" Sure enough it felt like skin that had a dozen hundred mosquito bites. I heard one of the girls squeal in the background, "Oooohh!" and he pulled the jeans back down.

"Hey Dave," one of the guys hollered. "We're gonna be setting up a game in about five." From the glazed looks passed along between the girls I guessed what the big game was—a neighbourhood version of War.

"Sure, I'm in. But I have to take it kind of easy. Hey, Mags, you gonna look after me? Make sure I don't get blown away?"

And so me and Dave were told to go off toward the park, the place where all the losers were sent to keep watch. And I guess we were the losers—the last drafts for the Soviet side.

My brothers were picked first for the American team, which sucked because the Americans always won. Park was kind of an ironic pet name, though. About the size of a dime, the park only had a bench, a few measly little trees, a rickety, rusted-up drinking fountain and swing set, and a patch of shit-stained grass surrounded by a whole lot of dirt.

We took cover behind the bench, stretching ourselves flat in the dirt. I don't know how long we were there, maybe half an hour, before a bunch of the guys kicked off their covert operations around our position, knocking each other out of the game. But me and Dave were bored. I mean, what the hell was the point of playing if no one could see you and no one bothered to look for you?

So we were going AWOL, slinking the best we could towards the trees, when there was this ear-splitting noise. It sounded like the sky was a pair of jeans being ripped up the crotch. I knew we were dead ducks anyhow, so I stopped for a minute. I looked up at the pink and purple clouds and there was this plane streaking so low it was practically grazing the buildings. I had to grab my ears to shut out the roar, but I watched as the belly flashed and winked silver at us and disappeared. The only thing left was this tag of white smoke. It just hung there in the sky like somebody's signature.

I was still watching this plane like an idiot when my brother Pete came out of nowhere, dangling down from a tree limb and took us out with his BB gun. Pop. Pop. Two quick shots, and he flipped down from the tree, saying, "Gotcha, meat," in his best Mr. T voice. Dave turned the colour of a purple popsicle. I couldn't figure out what his damage was. I mean, I'd been hit in the arm but I didn't think it was too bad. "You're such a fucking asshole, Pete," he said, and his eyes scrunched up like someone had kicked him in no man's land. "Couldn't you aim a little better?"

Pete shrugged, said, "Tough luck, buddy. War is hell," and slithered away to pop his next victim. We started back to the stoop—it was the holding pen for the deceased and p.o.w.'s— but every few minutes Dave stopped to massage his leg. I kept asking, "What's'a matter, Dave?" But he just shrugged and said, "Nothin. Nothin. Don't worry about it."

It was almost dark by the time we made it back. The shadow of our building swamped everything in sight and the air had a frosty bite to it. There were at least ten kids milling around, smoking and waiting for the game to end. Just a whole bunch of dead people, a few prisoners, some of them moaning, holding their sides or whatever, pretending to be wounded soldiers. Most of them had been picked off a lot sooner than us, which made me look pretty good. Our fear- less Russian leader Tim was there. He ruffled my hair, said, "Good game, kid," while Dave sat down and stretched out his bum leg.

Just then this kid Garret ran out of the building, pimply face flushed. "Holy shit. Ho-ly *shit*, man." And I mean he was spraying people he was so excited. "You won't believe what I just heard. The fucking Reds just shot down a Korean plane full of ci*vil*ians."

For a second I thought he was cracking up. I mean, I wasn't allowed to play with the guys very often but even I knew that we never pretended to have planes and shit. But then Tim got this look on his face, as if he'd just heard his mother got run over. "Oh my God," he said. "You shitting me?"

Just then the American team came in, leading the rest of our fallen comrades at gunpoint. "Bet you anything that's gonna be the thing. Kaboom! Reagan's totally going apeshit," Garret said. My brother Pete held his gun like the game was still on. "What the hell's your problem, Dave," he yelled.

"You know, you prick."

"C'mere and say that."

"I would if I could fucking stand up after what you did."

"What'd he do?" Tim asked.

"Fucking shot me right in the bad leg. I just got my cast off, for Christ's sakes."

"Crybaby," Pete said.

"I'd wipe the street with your ass for that mouth of yours, boy."

"I'd like to see you try."

Dave put weight on his cane like he was getting up. "Fuck you. I'm out of here."

"Watch it, Dave," my older brother Joe said. "I wouldn't mind fucking with you."

Meanwhile Dave stood up and limped over to me. He took my cheeks in his one hand, pinching them together, and kissed me. Hard. His face scratched my skin. His fingernails dug crescents into my cheeks. I tried to break away, thinking, what the hell was Dave mad at me for? What the hell did I do? Garret blathered away in the background like he didn't even notice what was going on. "Did ya hear? There's gonna be a war, man. Fucking World War Three." And my brother Joe: "You're so going to die, David. Get your hands off my sister." I felt Joe's hands prying Dave away from me.

Dave let me go all at once. Just dropped me flat. He didn't even look at me as he murmured, "See you 'round, Mags," and limped away, grabbing at his leg. Joe went after him and kicked him in the ass.

"Don't come back, you fucking dog. 'Less you really want to die." And I guess he didn't want to die. Because Dave took his chicken skin and went away, and I never saw him again.

This is my neighbourhood. It reminds me of a lover who was abandoned about a million years ago or an animal that wants to chew off its own leg. There's this: steam from sewers when it's cold, the wandering mew of sirens down the streets, the endless seedy shops and small, morose shop-keepers. The long necklace of cars parking and unparking along the sidewalks, glittering like rhinestones. There are buildings that loom and sidle up to the corners and curbs, darkening with smoke and exhaust as the lines around a women's eyes might accumulate—too early, not even in her prime. And then there are the things which connect all other things. There is the street, and another street, and it is these things that we crawl upon. And there are the outsiders, and the insiders, and everything in between is just love and war.

So me and PK find ourselves wandering into the heat of early afternoon. The city's on fire. PK walks with purpose down the long, main street filled with summer shoppers and tourists. This is the street where everything smells like car fumes and perfume, and every window is filled with some-thing expensive and beautiful. Vases and flowery cotton dresses. Leather couches and futons and shoes. This is the street where kids like us hang out. I ask PK, "Where are we going?"

"To the zoo," he tells me, and smiles.

Another block and we reach the patio of PK's zoo, high-lighted in front by a couple dozen choppers and other such machines. We grab a table, the only one left and of course without an umbrella. The bikes are lined up, lean and hun-gry, on the sidewalk display. A slight breeze picks up and blows against a Harley Davidson flag, its original black and orange bleached down to a fine matted grey on the back of a slick blue bike. The motorcycle's skin is flecked with silver, and it glows against the black leather of the seat. A tattooed helmet perches on top of the back rest.

"Long distance runners," PK mumbles. He says this every

time, and I let him repeat it over and over again. "Looonnng," he stretches out the syllables, "disssstance...."

We are enthralled by the colours, by the sound of an engine being turned over. The heaviness of the machines and their freedom. "Long distance runners," he says. "Like cross-country runners. Down into the states, maybe South America. Hampered by the ocean, of course, but it's a big enough continent."

"You thinking of picking one up?" I joke.

"Just thinking. Those bikes are like their legs, don't you think? You only see them walking to the patio. Or to the bar. Nothing else."

"Maybe to take a piss," I say, "or to buy a pack of cigarettes."

"Yeah, but you can get those at the bar, too."

This is their world, the long distance runners, and it seems important enough—watching their cartoon-banded arms flex and stretch, raising fresh glasses of beer to their faces. Foam wiped with the back of a hand from a battered moustache. One of the women with platinum hair and leather tank bra lets slip a vigorous giggle. They all breathe tough and tired in the heat, all of them and their bikes.

Somehow it's almighty important. The way we sit among them on the blazing plastic chairs, ignored and not even of age, being served cold beer. PK's glasses steam with heat, the muddy green of his eyes erased by the blinding white sun.

We sit on the patio, me and PK, just perusing the day away until Benny, or as he's sometimes known, 'Benzadrine', shows up with a pimply little street kid.

"So listen," Benny pulls up a chair, his eyes shuttered from his wake-and-bake joint. "So, I got to the corner and then I said to myself, hey, I know where the citizens will be. So I brought my new friend over, and then I saw you guys, and I said to myself, yeah." We motion to the empty chairs and the little street kid sits down. "Magpie, PK," Benny introduces with his head down and arms spread magnanimously, "this guy's gonna be hanging around for a while."

PK peers through his glasses, "What's your name, guy?"

"The guys at Derek's call him Spanky," Benny chimes in. In the time it takes to blink this kid is blushing like a rodeo clown and looking at his hands.

"You know Derek?" I ask. PK sits up in his chair, lowers his glaring glasses.

"I'm staying at his place for a few days."

PK's head nods up and down, "Is that Spanky with a 'y' or an 'i'?"

"Dunno," he says. "Guess a 'y'."

"That's real nice."

"Yeah, so anyways," Benny tosses his head from shoulder to shoulder, "where the hell is that bitch Janine? I want a beer, goddamn it."

"Cool it, you fucker. It's busy today, in case you haven't noticed," I say. "What are you on today?"

"I ain't on nothin', bitch," he grins and runs a hand through his dark messy hair.

Benny's the only person who gets away with calling me names. It's a game for us, and even so, if my brothers are around, Benny cleans up his mouth. Nobody calls me nothing when my brothers are around, and they're around a whole lot. But Benny gets away with just about everything else. He thinks he's the updated version of The Fonz, and not just because he's good-looking, which he is in a naked sort of way. Brown slits of eyes in a body that has that permanent tan thing going. He's got the look of an ex-con—tight, wiry muscles and tattoos. No one wants to be on Benny's bad side because he's always jacked up. But I fool with Benny because

I know he isn't as dumb as he looks, and therefore I'm as good as safe no matter what. Benny doesn't have a death wish. I'll stop bugging him when he does.

We may not like Benny but we sure like to know him. He's done guest bouncing appearances at all of the clubs, knows everybody, and sells everybody drugs. And so Benny's asking, "So, you guys need anything for tonight? Maybe a little hash oil that I just got?" PK shakes his head no, and Benny starts going off on a tangent, telling these bald-faced lies about this blushing kid. He laughs and says, "Spanky's on the lam, actually. He just discovered his parents were Nazi conspirators last month," when Janine the barwench comes by.

"What the fuck, Benny," she opens.

"What the fuck yourself, ho," he says in his best pimp imitation. He pulls Janine with the boob job and the badly permed hair onto his lap. "So honey," he nuzzles her, "you gonna be my date tonight or what?"

She giggles back at him, "Sure, but bring some coke or somethin', eh. God knows you're not good for anything else." He smacks her ass as she shimmies off his lap, and he yells after her, "And bring us a pitcher of beer, woman!" This is how it goes for us: the beer runneth over, Benny lyeth through his teeth and showeth off, the littlest hobo friend a-blushing. And there's me, and there's PK, and there's the long distance runners.

It gets to be about six, I guess. The shadows on the patio swagger closer to our table. Benny leaps up and says, "Well, folks, show's over. I gotta be at my business." And then he yells across the patio, "See you at the Underground, baby," to Janine, who's serving three pitchers to a table full of bikers. And he leaves this new kid, Spanky, behind.

"Well, Spanky my friend," PK begins once Benny has finished his rounds, "looks like Alfalfa has left the episode.

Tune in for our next installment when Bonzo drives to Vegas." The kid blushes again and curls his fingers around the half-pint glass. Fragile hands. He's got the look of a child in his hands, the kind that are sort of puffy and sweet that you imagine to be sticky but soft as a cat's fur.

"Do you know Benny real well?" I ask. I'm being careful because I can't believe Benny just ditched this poor-ass kid. Spanky shakes a head of dirty tentacles at us.

"How old are you?"

He clears his throat. "Sixteen." But I'm doubtful, thinking more like fourteen, fifteen.

"How long you been here? Not long, eh?"

He starts to look all alarmed, says, "How did you know? Two months, I think. Three? It's June, right?"

"Uh huh."

We always know the outsiders from the in. There's a look to a newcomer, as if we can see their fragile skins being covered over by a new, more leathery growth. But I don't want him to think it means anything to us, so I say, "PK and I are going out tonight. You wanna hang? Derek's probably coming."

"Sure." Spanky twists his fingers, pulling on them until they pop one by one.

"The thing I don't get," PK's musing away, "is why Derek didn't tell us about you."

And this kid says, "Maybe Derek's afraid of what people think. About his being nice, I mean."

Yeah, that's Derek. PK grins like he's just found another kindred spirit. Spanky just keeps looking at his fingertips, blushing with his greasy head down. That's Derek all right, and Derek isn't nice to very many people. Derek is the kind of guy who will join in a street scrap just because he wants to 'flex'. He's the kind of guy you worry might beat up his parole officer, or his girlfriend—or any guy who looked twice at her. But when he's nice—well, you have to be pretty special for Derek to go out on a limb for you. Our esteem for Spanky went up and up.

The whole gang pretty much got the same feeling as soon as they saw him. Gosh, this kid. That warm, rising slide in your throat, making you almost want to cry, eyes watering despite yourself when he does something sort of sweet and quiet. And it isn't just that he's a good guy. Even after some time on the streets he's not all sullen the way some people get. He doesn't think the world owes him. It's as if Spanky knows God as a personal friend, and anything dark giving him the evil eye can just keep on looking.

It's times like these, though, when everything starts to feel flat and depressed, when you start to think about the bastards who are actually more unfortunate than yourself. Spanky gets up, says as if he's been at a cocktail party, "It was nice to meet you both. I'll see you later," all the while looking at his nasty sneakers that are unravelling red at the toes.

"Meet us at the Underground later," PK tells him. "If anyone gives you a hassle at the door, ask for a guy named Jackson and tell him who you are. 'Kay?"

Spanky nods, walks away. As if he hasn't a care in the world. He could be a Gap poster boy in disguise. Packed in a delicate air, that Spanky. But delicate means destructible where we live. Delicate doesn't last long.

My best friend has always been a bit of a freak of nature. I laid eyes on PK for the first time in grade four. It was the first day of school. The bell rang and we filed inside the portable that looked like it belonged in a white-trash trailer park. It was a typical kind of first day: all the kids the same—whiny and pretty much clueless. I remember looking around, thinking I'd see Nick-the-dick Stanistopolous beside me, but he wasn't there. Instead there was this quiet kid whose nose was running a bit and leaving a shiny snail trail under his nostrils. Funny looking. Big round glasses and kinky hair that stood up all over the place, curling into these beautiful round waves at the tips. The kind of hair that every little girl wants. So this kid is just sitting there, looking around every now and then. Then he reaches into a beat-up little bag and pulls out a book. The craziest thing—and it wasn't any *Spot Jane and Dick* deal or *Charlie and the Chocolate Factory* like most of the kids would read, if at all. It was an honest to goodness real book. The thick kind without pictures. This kid just buried his long nose right in it and ignored everything else. And then Miss White called his name for attendance.

"Pick. Peck. Ahm. Mr. Douglas—?"

The class was silent, craning their heads around looking for this mysterious guy who was about to catch major shit. And thirty seconds later all 33 eyes were on this oblivious guy.

"Mister—augh—Douglas. Will you be joining us any time soon?"

Nothing.

"Mr. Douglas." She was really pissed at this point. Every time Miss White was pissed she stood up and slammed her little hand down on the desk.

He finally raised his eyes to meet hers. He gave her this look, all serious, and said without a hint of sass or anything, "I'm sorry. I just wanted to finish this page."

"This is no way to make a good impression at your new school, Mr. Douglas." She sashayed from behind the desk in her wide skirt and came down the aisle toward him. "Now what would be so very interesting that you can't participate in class," she said, and you could tell she wanted so badly for the book to be a porn mag or something. I mean, her eyes were lighting up. Before she could grab it PK had the bookmark back into it and offered it up.

"It's very good, Ma'am," he said in this quiet, serious voice. "Do you know this author?" I got chills up and down my back. The room was so quiet you could hear the dropping of IQ points. Everyone was sucking in their breath, wondering what the hell 'ma'am' meant, waiting to see what colour the fireworks were going to be. She studied the cover for a second or two, and I watched as the telltale frown began between her eyebrows, stretched over her forehead and drooled down her mouth.

"Mr. Douglas," she snarled, and we all knew what was coming. "I don't find this to be a very amusing joke."

"I'm sorry, Miss White. I'm afraid I don't understand."

She snorted a little, pushed her bangs back out of the way of her frown. "I tell you it's not funny. I don't know what kind of practical joke you're trying to play here, Mr. Douglas—"

"With all due respect, Ma'am," he said, and wiped at the shiny patch beneath his nose with one of his sleeves. "It's not the first time I've read it."

And I thought it so funny, so amazing, because Miss White just pulled herself up real straight. She took a long look at PK, and then she handed him the book and walked away muttering, "Pay attention." Sure, her hands kept fluttering up and down her neck, smoothing her skirt, but she didn't do anything. It was as if he'd told her that Santa Claus was real or something, and she just had to go along with it. I mean, what was she going to do? Usually the kids in my class had to be paid just to keep from selling their books. Literacy wasn't exactly a high priority. And PK didn't seem to mind all the kids gaping at him. He didn't even seem to notice.

I couldn't get him alone until the next day at recess. I

caught him hanging out on the front steps of the school with his nose buried in that book. I stood there staring like a stupid idiot. I don't even know what I wanted from him. I guess I was curious. And it might have been a good five minutes before he noticed me and pulled his head out of the book, and I found that to be pretty crazy, too. He obviously wasn't afraid of getting beaten on for reading.

"What's your name?" I asked him.

"PK."

"What's it stand for."

"Does it matter?" He was so serious. It cracked me up.

"Yeah."

"Why?"

"It just does, that's all. I'll tell you what my name stands for if you'll tell me yours."

"Okay. What's your name?"

"Magpie."

"Really?" His eyes got all big and round behind those glasses. Big and interested.

"Well, it's not my *real* first name. You first."

"Pekoria. My mam had me in a town called Pekoria. She keeps saying she was so relieved it was over and we could get out of there she called me by the name of the town. So she'd never forget not to go back or something. But I think it's kind of girly. I think she wanted me to be a girl."

"Oh, well, y'know, I kinda like that name. PK's a tough name. That's good."

"Yeah," he said. When he talked to me he was real intense, as if he could stare straight through a person's eyeballs. But they were great eyes—like a bowl full of trees and flecks of brown for the branches. Quiet eyes. Eyes that I could trust. "Now you," he said.

I bit my lip, squeezed my eyes shut. "Mary Margaret."

Then I gave him my best 'I'll kick your ass if you tease me' look. "Don't you dare call me that. Even if you're mad at me. Only the teachers and my mother call me that. And pretty soon," I bragged, "when I'm old enough, not even the teachers will call me that."

"Mary's not a bad name."

"Naw, but it's wimpy. Magpie's a better name. My brothers named me that."

We spent a few moments sizing each other up. He was obviously one of us. I mean, he had that tattered look about him. His shirt was too big, out of fashion. It was one of those polyester deals like right out of *Battlestar Galactica*. His runners were about as beat-up as runners could be. The rubber soles flopped off the toes like half-dead fish.

"Hey," I said. "Can I see that book you're reading?"

"Sure." He carefully placed the bookmark in and handed it to me. It was huge, thick with the scent of many pages. For a second I was confused, thinking it was a comic book or something. I mean, the only thing on the cover was a giant worm. "*Dune*'s a great book," he said. "Do you know it?"

"Naw. What's it about? Looks gory."

"Yup, it's kinda gory. But not how you probably think. Y'see," he said, "it's sort of all about a family dynasty but not really. See, there's this prince guy way in the future who's going to meet his fate." And PK talked all through recess about witches, witch babies, desert people who ride worms and have blue, blue eyes. Murders and mayhem. It was obvious we both got off on this little cultural exchange. What a trip it was, hanging out with this kid who had a whole other world kicking around in his head. A whole other place that wasn't our hood.

So PK goes, "You think too much, Mags."

We're back at Livin' Easy after the Bull, trying to sober up over a can of Spaghetti-o's before a solid night's drinking. Olivia Newton John is getting physical on the Disney turntable.

"Nooo. You think too much, Peek. I think too little but profoundly. Hand me that cig, won't ya?" He tosses me a half-full pack of Players and collapses on the bed. There's one lit in his hand and it's a mountain of ash at this point. I have to resist the urge to run under it with an outstretched hand, like trying to catch a baby thrown out of a burning building. But then he sits up, scattering the ashes all over the dank blue hospital sheet.

"What the hell is up with you today, anyhow? You're being all quiet and female on me today."

"Shut up, nerd. I'm busy here." I hand him the ashtray, which he ignores.

"Yeah. I've been thinking too. Education, Mags." He says this so suddenly. It's one of those great conversations that happens entirely in PK's head but he expects me to know what's going on.

"Uhm, yeah?" I say. He stops talking for a while, just looks up into the smoke like he's reading it as he stands up and puts another record on.

"Whaddaya think of the Bee Gees?"

"Okay. Just no more Shaft today, alright?"

"Fine."

"Get on with it." My hands spin, trying to hurry him up. But I know what's going to happen: he sits himself down slowly, still churning it around until I think I'll have to smack him to get it out.

"We have to stop skipping so many classes," he finally says. My jaw drops.

"Excuse me?"

"I mean next year. It'll be our last. We should make it good."

"What the hell are you talking about, Peek? It's *been* good. It's been the best. Why fuck with something that ain't broken?"

"Grades, Mags. We don't try. We should try."

"What the hell are you worried about your grades for, dip-shit? You're one of the smartest fucki—"

"University. Scholarships."

"You're forgetting one important thing, Peckoria. I ain't goin' to college. You know that."

PK just grins at me, slapping his leg like someone's just told a dirty joke. "Why so negative? There's always a way. It's just a matter of a little ingenuity and robbing a few banks."

"Okay. That's it. Reality check time."

"Magpie, look at us. We could get out of this. We could see what life's like on the other side."

"I don't much like stepping through glass."

"We're smart. We read at college levels."

"You read at college levels, Peek. I read the Coles Notes." I smoke my cigarette down to the filter, smash it into the tray and pull another one from the pack. PK watches in awe and disgust as I light it. "PK," I say, blowing out all of the air inside me. "You're the smart one. I can barely keep up when I'm trying. You and I both know they only let about one in every 17 million poor kids go to school on scholarships. And frankly, I don't feel like taking on all those loans just so I can be more poor than I already am. I give you my blessings, alright? Go to class, go to University. You should be there. They'll probably stick you in a think tank or some shit." He shakes his curly head at me, and then I feel like I have to level with him. "I know you'll figure it out and all, but you know it takes total brains to get out that way. Brains and an open wallet. At least you've got one of those."

"You never know, right? Just promise me to think about

it. And we'll stop skipping so many classes."

"I'm not even sure I want out. What's the point, right? They're just going to find a way to fuck us."

PK snorts and opens his beat-up copy of *Nausea* and starts reading it upside down. I close my eyes a bit and the room has this magnet pull. It's pulling me in circles. Or maybe that's just gravity. Whatever it is I feel like I'm falling out of the ride right about now.

"PK?"

"Yeah. What."

"I'm kinda freaked about something."

"What've you got to be freaked about, besides the usual gang-turf wars, homeless psychopaths, murders of passion, priests who like little boys—or in your case little tomboys. Acid rain? The market price of coke?"

"Come on," I say, laughing louder than I should have, "be serious for a minute."

"Wasn't that serious enough for you?"

"Stop being a smartass."

"If you keep looking at things the way they are you'll just get swallowed up, Mags. You have to think of the possibilities of things. For instance," he pauses, looking over towards the sink, "did you know that companies have quotas for how many bugs and paint chips are allowed in any given can of Spaghetti-o's? You can get your entire day's worth of protein eating the bug fragments in there. Think about it—we could both get a job at the Spaghetti-o's factory counting bug parts per cubic inch of volume."

I reach over and pull the Bee Gees off Disney, watching the little blue disc thing swirl around and around. Neil Diamond goes on and I turn the volume way up.

"That's not what I'm talking about."

"But we could get loads of freebies, Mags. Think about it."

"Peek—"

"What? Okay. What're you talking about then?"

"My mom. Fran did the weirdest thing yesterday."

"Fran?" PK acts all mock surprise. "Our Franny? Little Frances Smith? I don't believe it."

"Pee Kay."

"Alright, alright. Well? Are you going to tell me about it or are we going to play charades."

"You got that from a movie."

"So what? It's still a good line." He turns the volume down again. I can see the nicotine stains on his skinny-ass fingers from here.

"She sat me down yesterday morning and started going on the strangest trip."

PK's head shoots up. "What kind of stuff?"

"Like, woman stuff, I guess."

"God, more of this female crap?"

When my mother came and sat down it was like looking at one of her old photos: primped and starched and sad. I was looking at her and I thought, God, she's an old woman already. It was the way she did it—carefully bending at the hips, placing herself just so on the plastic-covered kitchen chair. Intently stirred her coffee.

"Give me one of those cigarettes, Mary Margaret," she says. I swear I almost spit my coffee out right then.

"Sure Mom." I light a cigarette and hand it to her. She inhales real deep and make the tip glow all bright orange like a jack o'lantern. Everything comes out all lame: "I didn't know you smoked."

"I didn't know you smoked either," she lowers her eyebrows and growls. But then instead of the lecture she just smokes quietly for a while. "I used to smoke, you know.

Before you were born. We didn't know any better back then."
She cracks her mouth open and lets the smoke out in one big
gust. It's an ugly smile, too gray, too awful with her life.
"Now, don't take off—I want to talk to you about a thing or
two before you go off terrorizing the city today."

"I swear I didn't do it. It was probably Pete. You know
what a slob he is—"

"Now just shut yer trap before I lose my temper. If I don't
get this out now I may never say it. So just sit there and listen
for a minute."

I think it was something in her voice that stopped me. Or
maybe it was the wild, fixed look in her eyes. It wasn't pretty
at all. But it was more alive than I'd seen Fran in a long time.
And then she says to the smoke that's crawling its way up to
the cracked plate over the light fixture, "Did you know that
this is a special anniversary?"

Back then, now. It's always the same. Trouble for us has
always been like that annoying dinner guest that shows up
early, eats too much and stays late. I was still a baby when my
dad left—four or five, I think. And my mother, from that time
on, was a total wreck. I mean, she didn't even have a high
school diploma or a driver's license. Three kids on her own,
nothing but her own two hands to save us from the poor-
house, as she likes to tell it.

I don't really remember when he left. I have these half-
formed impressions, like the shadows that creep around the
ceiling when you're a kid. I know that my mother was young
when she married him and old when he left. I love looking
at pictures of her as a young woman, though. Her hair all
curled, the colour of a copper kettle. Slender, smiling. So
pretty. Underneath every picture there'd be a caption, as if it
made the photo more real: 'Frances O'Connor, age—'.

Later captions read, 'Fran O'Connor Smith and Billy Smith,' only the side with my father has been ripped away. I'm left with his hands curled ominously around my mother's waist. A hairy hand, a patch of blue dress shirt. If she catches me sifting through them she mutters under her breath, "I should've known better than to marry a Scot."

She worked herself to the bone as a cleaning lady. She cleaned people's houses, took a bus to get there in the early hours of the morning and came back late and exhausted. Not once did I ever hear a word about that life, her job. All I knew was that she'd never pick me up and give me a squeeze. Her back hurt too much. She began to smell like floor wax and vacuum cleaner dust, and that became her familiar smell, the one I associate with her and her alone. Her knees: patches of dry, permanently stained, blotchy red skin. Her fingers: chapped right down to the ends of her yellowed nails. Looking at her hands I always hear this one song in my head: *Work your fingers to the bone, what do you get? Boney fingers, boney fingers.*

Our lives were a series of moves whenever we couldn't pay the rent for three consecutive months. That meant a new apartment every six to eight months. Boxes were squashed into new corners and closets and went unpacked for years at a time. My brothers would take the day off school to help my mother move everything, and then they picked me up from school and brought me to our new 'home'. Every time we moved Fran would cry as she tried to wipe the stains from the new walls, the grimy hand prints left by several dozen previous tenants. The way she saw it, she didn't have to live in a sty no matter how cheap the rent, not if she was still breathing long enough to clean it up. So she scrubbed and scrubbed, desperate to peel those marks from the wall, to erase punctures from doors and dented walls.

Pete and Joe were my mother's little men, and she certainly made them work for that title. They had to pick me up from school, make sure I was dressed in the morning, that I had a lunch or knew how to get it off someone else. It was their responsibility to spit in my hair, to knock me down when I whined. I boxed them in our tiny bedroom that the three of us shared, to get my stuff back. I wrestled them for hand-me-downs and their abandoned toys. They made me fight for the right to exist. But that I understood: I accepted that, even if I resented it. I knew, too, that they'd beat the hell out of anyone who tried to touch me. It was their right to hurt me, no one else's, and there was an odd sort of comfort in that.

The year I met PK my mother started cleaning the Catholic Church in our neighbourhood, the grandest thing around. Supposedly it was our church, too, our faith, but I never got around to being religious. The domed ceiling rang like a four-alarm fire set by God Himself every Sunday and twice a day for first communions, baptisms, weddings and funerals. It was a good sound, familiar and practically wholesome. Father Wallace started coming by around the same time. He was the new priest, the guy who took over when Father Thomas had a heart attack in the middle of Easter mass. He was the one who gave my mother her new job.

We moved into another apartment and stayed put ever since. All the same, it took us two and a half years to get around to unpacking the last of the boxes. It was a slow process of faith. My brothers and I kept the cardboard folded up and packed into our closets for another two years.

My mother would have Father Wallace over for supper in our new, super-clean apartment with only a few holes. She let her auburn hair slip down over her shoulders, brushed out and fanned across her neck. She put on her nice dress, the one with the blue stripes that made her eyes a deep blue. She dabbed her carefully hoarded Charlie perfume on her wrists.

Father Wallace would come knocking on the door. He didn't even have to buzz up—people saw him coming and just let him in. A scowling Joe or Pete would open up. Father Wallace always ruffled their hair, even though they were almost as tall as him by then. He'd grin at me, the big dimple in the middle of his chin practically winking at me, give me candy and tell me what a pretty little girl I was turning into. My mother blushed away in her corner of the kitchen, proud that she could serve him the best roast beef in the neighbourhood now that things were looking up.

So PK goes, "Spill it, Mags. Why all the secrecy? You know how much I love to hear about this shit."

"We were just talking, right? And then she turned to me all serious-like and goes—"

"—And goes, 'Actually, your father's not dead, he's really the dog-faced man.'"

"She started up on me."

"Yeah. And?"

"No, I mean it, Peek. It was weird."

PK turns back to his upside-down Sartre.

"Like she was afraid something bad was going to happen. Like about not following in my brothers' footsteps. That whole 'get a life' thing. That kind of stuff."

"You're kidding, right? Your mother said that? Our Franny?"

"Yeah. Like I said. It was kinda like hearing a graduation speech from the terminally insane. What do you think?"

"Is she sick?" I take his book and throw it at his head. But I throw like a girl, so it misses and catches his shoulder.

"No!"

"Then maybe she's just feeling her age."

"For Christ's sake, PK. She's barely pushing forty."

"Yeah," he says, hitching his eyebrows up and wiggling them, "but she certainly looks old."

"Be serious."

"Give me details."

I light up again, fingering PK's blue sheet, and try to imagine what it was like to love my two brothers the way Fran did. Fanatically. Fearfully.

"They're going to leave, you know."

"Who? Who, Mom?"

"Who the hell d'you think? Peter and Joseph. Soon."

"Naw. They'll kick around for a while yet. I think they actually like the service around here." I get up and pour Fran and myself more coffee. Stir in the milk and sugar the way Fran likes it.

"They're grown-up. They'll want to start up families soon."

I snort, "They probably already have. Several by now, I'd say."

"Watch your mouth, Mary Margaret."

"Yes, Mom." She takes another cigarette from my pack and I watch her unpractised hands fumble with the lighter.

"You're going to be all alone."

"No I'm not. I've got PK. And you. And besides, no matter where they go Joe and Pete'll look out for me. Their reputation alone will keep me safe till I'm grey."

"Don't be stupid, girl. You can't live on a reputation," she scoffs. "What if I'm not around, Maggie? I'm not going to be around forever. And your brothers," she sighs. Her lips pucker when she sighs. "What if they're thrown in jail? Humm?"

I think my jaw must have dropped through the table,

because Fran gives me that whole 'I'm-so-cynical-as-if-I-didn't-know' smirk. "Come on, Mary Margaret," she says. "I may be old and tired and uncool, but I'm not stupid."

A cigarette unfolds into my hand. I stare at it as if I'd pulled a rabbit from a hat.

"I also know you're a good girl. I know that you keep out of trouble. Mostly." I think I actually start smiling. "Whether it's due to your brothers or that friend of yours, I'm not sure. But I'm proud of you. Even if you do look ridiculous."

"Gee, thanks, Mom."

"All the same," she says, " that'll help about as much as a kick in the arse."

"Excuse me?"

"I would say maybe you should get married, let your husband look after you. But that sort of thing doesn't seem to work any more," she snorts. "You can't rely on a man. And it'll be hard on your own, too."

"Mom, I'll be fine. Really. I'll get a job and—"

"I want better for you than I had." Her face reddens just below her eyes and around the tops of her cheeks, like it always does when she's getting upset. "I think about you wandering around like one of those bag ladies."

"It's okay, Mom. I'll be okay."

"It's different for your brothers," she says. "They're men. They can always get something that'll pay better even though they've never gotten the grades you have. They aren't as smart as you."

"Mom!"

She shrugs, remembers her cigarette and puffs. "Well it's true."

"Well you don't have to be all sexist about it," I say. "I can get a job."

"You know what it's like, my little girl. You know what it's like out there. Just walking down the street at night."

"Come on, Mom. No one bothers me. Never. Ever."

"Ahh, but you don't know. You're brothers can't protect you from everything. And if they move away, or get put in jail. Or die, God forgive me." Fran crosses herself melodramatically, her eyes upturned to the cracks on the ceiling.

"Don't talk that way."

"I'm going to tell you something that my mother once said to me, when I was about your age. About to marry your father. She said to me, 'Are you really considering the future, Frances?' I didn't know what the hell she was talking about. I always thought getting all set up was the thing, eh? That's what we did back then."

The image of my grandmother floats there in the face of my mother. The same tired presence, a life that has been too long and too sad. "I believed in it all. I was pious. Do the best you can in the eyes of God and man and the future will take care of itself. I thought that's what we women were supposed to do." She hoots, slaps her thigh. Shakes her head.

"Now?" she says. "Now I don't think so. You have to step lightly, Mary Margaret, because otherwise you'll just get stepped on. You've got to think about the future, my girl. Doing what you're supposed to gets you nowheres. You've got to be smart about it, girl. You've got to watch on all sides and get a leg up out of this hole. "

"Fran—" I start, "Mom."

"The rich keep getting richer and we keep getting poorer. I didn't need no school to tell me that." Her accent kicks in strongly at times like this, her sweet up and down trill.

"I'm going to be okay, Mom. We take care of our own."

"These are not your own, Mary Margaret! I wish to God I'd had somewheres to send you. Some money," she grabs my hand. I feel her squeeze all the bones together like an elastic that pulls all the skin. "Promise me you'll try, you'll just try to get out of this."

"I promise," I say, but I don't feel it. I'm panicking. Caffeine rushes through my limbs and pounds on my skull. Fran lights yet another cigarette, and her awful smile comes out again. Her gums are dark around the edges of her teeth.

"A special day," she says. "This was the day your father left all those years ago." My mother's eyes are hard and watery and blue today, like a lake that's sunk itself into stone. They have the look of the surgeon's knife about them—precise and willing to cut out all the bullshit. "Be careful, Mary Margaret. Keep your eyes peeled, eh?"

Underground

Rule one, I'd say, is something about having to belong. Jackson stands at the door, smoking one of a never-ending chain of butts as PK and I walk up. He's built kind of like a Mack truck. Big shoulders, pumped chest, legs like tree trunks and only a slight bulge in his stomach where the beer sits. I mean, the guy's impressive-looking. A true body-building type, Jackson, even though every time I see him I think he's just come out of detox. Jackson's interesting in the way he's older, quiet. Long streaks of gray shine through his shoulder-length locks, and his whiskers grow in colourless chunks. Hell, even his eyes are gray. Jackson is, of course, the Underground's infamous bouncer.

I'm only seventeen, mind you, and PK's only eighteen. We don't even have fake ID to flash to a bouncer if the cops were to show up. But they let us take our chances, and they theirs. I walk up to the door first. Jackson's looking the other way, down the street where there are some hooting jocks. "Fucking meatheads," I hear him mumble under his breath, and then I stretch up on my tiptoes, lace my fingers over Jackson's eyes.

"Guess who?"

"Umh. Jimmy fucking Carter. Elvis. My mother." Jackson's low voice tumbles out of his body and his fingers brush across my knuckles.

"That's right, Jackson. I'm yo' mama."

"Well you're short enough. Uhhhh. Short. Magpie."

"I should kick your ass for that," I say as he turns around.

"How're you doing, sweetie," he says. I get picked up like a sack of potatoes and cinched into a bear hug.

"You miss me, Jackson?"

"Yeah. Where you been."

"Finals."

"Where's PK?"

"Right here," Peek pops up from around the corner of the club door. He's wearing this shit-eating grin, and I think it's for Jackson when I spy a group of kids coming up to the door. They're the giggling, fresh variety, wearing all their club clothes and hair gel. Spandex, polyester pants and shirts and tight, high skirts. The kind of kids that think shopping for their club clothes at Club Monaco is way cool. Jackson throws a tree trunk arm across the door and PK's grin balloons.

"'Whoa. Where's your ID?"

The kids, seven in all, start to groan and search through their pockets and purses. I'd say only three or four of them, tops, can be legal. Jackson works them, looking at their pictures as if he's a customs inspector. The front, the back, scratches the tops, holds the licenses up to the light.

"This is fake," he says to the youngest of the bunch. He's this kid who looks younger than me, if that's possible. More than that, though, he looks like a real pain in the ass. He's got the appearance of one of those rich and whiny minors who gets completely trashed and pukes all over his designer sweater and then starts picking fights. This is confirmed when he opens his big stupid mouth and says, "Come on, maaaan. Give us a break."

Jackson hates that more than anything. Don't call him 'man', I want to say. You don't even know the dude. "Come on yourself," Jackson waves his giant paw. "Fuck off."

The kids start yelling outside the door, at Jackson, at each other. The whole, "what are we going to do we promised sally ann or muffy we'd meet her here and her new boyfriend biff and oh mi god did you see what that girl was wearing?"—as if this is going to gain them sympathy points. I'd like to kick all their asses. These are the kids from school whose parents buy them cars for their high school graduation. These are the kids who come in and take over everything. If they were allowed to, they'd take over our club, too. But it's not going to happen. Some things are sacred.

Just as Jackson is waving the kids away and us in, PK shoots out, "Jackson. There's a new guy coming tonight. Staying with Derek. Shy-looking kid, about yay tall. They call him Spanky. Will you look out for him?"

"Mhmp," he nods. "I been hearing about this kid."

"Thanks, Jackson," I say, and kiss him on the cheek.

"Have fun kids," he waves like a sappy game show host. "Oh, Magpie, your brothers are here." The club kids are glaring daggers at our underage asses, but we float through that magic door coated in band posters and announcements. Up the carpet stairs worn down and putrid from a thousand heaving stomachs. PK in his black shorts frayed at the knee and favourite Dead Kennedys' 'Holiday in Cambodia' t-shirt. I in my boots, black 'Death to the Pixies' tee and a little skirt. My new hair, a brilliant shade of blue that matches my eyes piles up in an endless knotted mass. The Peekster and the Magpie.

My brothers introduced me to the scene for the first time on my fifteenth birthday at this very club. It was PK, Joe and Pete, their best friend Zach, and me. They took me around, Joe and Pete, introducing me to everyone like we were celebrities. They talked to the bouncers, the bartenders, the night manager, the busboys. There was the typical ruffling of hair, Joe telling them to remember me and keep me out of trouble. It was treated like a joke, really, but we all knew Joe was being completely serious. No one fucks with Joe, so no one was going to fuck with me. It was like a debutante ball for the youngest member of the mob, and everyone was obliged to treat me well. I suppose they could have been uncool about it, but when I think back—and I've been coming to the club ever since—maybe they were actually glad to add to the ranks. It's a matter of respect, really. And everyone seems to know which people will act properly, and the people who won't are shown how to fuck themselves.

That first night everything was on Joe, Pete, and the bartenders. We got, for lack of better words, wasted. Tequila shots, JD and coke, pitchers of beer. Seriously pissed. We drank like it was going out of style. PK and I had our first taste of moshing in a club pit and Joe and Pete and Zach sat back and laughed until they pissed themselves. Then Joe took us to the back room, the one where you needed VIP access to smoke joints without getting kicked out.

In my completely shitfaced haze I didn't really pay attention to the woman who'd shown up and was hanging all over Joe—well, to be fair Joe was hanging all over her, too. Joe never brought anyone home, but Pete had hinted that there was a girlfriend around. An actual serious relationship in our family? Unheard of. But then Joe was in front of me, I was weaving all over the place, and there was this woman. Eileen. Cute in a curly blond kinda way, freckles, big eyes. She wasn't a skank—the make-up was subtle, unlike the girls that Joe usually hung with who just threw everything and the kitchen sink on their pale, washed-out faces. Not really my cup of tea, though—she was too clean-looking, especially beside Joe in his thick leather jacket and pants. But he was obviously crazy about her. Held a hand at her back, bought her drinks, even kept Zach and Pete at a safe distance.

"Eileen, this is my sister Magpie."

"Nice to finally meet you, Magpie. Your brothers talk about you constantly."

"Yeah, well, I hope you got the cleaned-up version. Filthy-mouthed buggers."

Her freckles stretched out on her nose when she smiled, I thought. Or maybe it was the tequila. When she shot out her hand to shake mine it was a milky galaxy afloat with a million orange stars.

"They really adore you, you know. You're a lucky girl to have brothers like them."

Joe leaned in, his face covered in a soft, silly grin. The kind of smile that looks like a bout of gas is behind it. "Magpie, I want you and Eileen to be friends. Talk to her about all that girly shit if you need to. Right, Eileen?"

"Yeah," she said. She looked like the Madonna right then, all sort of lit up by the club lights and of course my head was spinning, and her galaxy arms and her teeth like white velvet patches in her mouth. And of course I was surprised that Joe would even think of such a thing. Or maybe, I thought, it was Eileen's idea. Joe probably felt real sad about me because we couldn't bother Fran. I was pretty much on my own and my best friend was a boy. Besides, there was all this unspoken stuff with my brothers and me, history we couldn't shake.

Joe was the oldest, a full six years older than me, and Pete was four older. Joe was our leader, the one who pretty much kept it all together after our dad skipped out. Every couple of weeks until Fran started cleaning the church he took Pete and me to this building. It was a long walk—about forty minutes each way—so he made sure we were wearing the shoes with the least holes and at least three sweaters. We usually didn't have enough for the bus fare, but even then I'm not sure we would have taken the bus.

The place was one of those typical warehouse-style places where the third floor's all boarded up and dark. The old windows sagged under dirt-crusted and chipped green paint. The door opened onto a floor like the kind you'd see in a roller rink. Cement and clean, with that peculiar rush of cool air curling off it. For the longest time I was under the illusion that it was some kind of discount grocery store that we'd somehow lucked in to having coupons for. There were all these people strolling around these long tables heaped with food, and the lady with the orange hair would come over, as she did every time.

"Hello, Joseph. How are things?"

Her name was Marge. I never quite got the story of how she and Joe met, or even what her job was exactly. I only know that we would go, and Joe would answer her, "Yep, it's okay." And at that Marge would walk us down the aisles of Kraft Dinner mountains, canned meats, red labelled mounds of beets and beans. Row upon row of corn syrup, Spam and powdered milk.

At the other end there were piles of boxes and bags filled up and ready to go. Marge would stroll us down there, point to a box or two for us to take home. Then we'd be all loaded down, and he'd set the box down and tell Pete and me to watch it while he walked off with Marge. They would be all deep in conversation for a few minutes, and sometimes I would see her hand snake out and grab Joe's shoulder and squeeze it. Sometimes I even saw her slip him some money. He'd shake his head but she would argue with him until he stuck it into his pocket. Then he'd come back to us, saying over his shoulder, "See you around, Marge," and she'd stand there, hands on her thick motherly hips, until we were out the door. She'd be smiling at us, her teeth large and even and white. They reminded me of pictures of racehorses—clean and strong and always winners.

When he was telling me to talk to Eileen I knew he was thinking of times like that. I know he hated those cardboard boxes more than anything on the planet. I know how much he resented having to look after us sometimes, having to find ways to get us food. No one who's been there ever forgets how it feels—like everything is slipping down, spiralling, and there's nothing to hold on to. I know it tore him up when he thought about how much we didn't have. I'm sure it felt a lot like hate.

I was such a stupid kid I didn't really understand that we were poor. I mean, I could tell the difference between kids from our hood and kids from a better one, but I wasn't really aware of the broken windows and glass littered around the tenement steps. I didn't know what it meant. It all kind of crept up on me when PK and I were going to the mall this one time. We were sitting at the front of the bus, where the seats all face inward, when Trish got on two stops later. We'd played rope games together, she and I and a bunch of other girls, at this one building I lived in. I think I'd even eaten at her apartment before. She had one of those perfume-making play sets and all the girls used to wait in the parking lot for her to bring it down so we could all have a crack at making a glamourous *eau de toilette*, with a far-out name like 'Gardenia' or 'Jasmine'.

I thought Trish was a looker. Great big, round, clear eyes, sweet and downy curly hair. She got on and said hello, asked what we'd been up to. Her mouth cracked open and shut as she talked. She was sucking on an orange lollipop, smiling. I mean, she was probably thinking she was beautiful, too. But her teeth were brown and yellow and black, rotting out of her mouth at age fourteen. Her clothes stretched across her thick, developed breasts in these tight, stained layers. Some of the people around us were staring at her, at us. This old lady was sneering. Some preppie kids in crappy designer jackets and shoes rolled their eyes at each other. This old guy with a cane stared at us like we were going to steal his wallet. And I mean, these people rode the bus. They couldn't have been all that rich themselves. But it was there, and it was real. It was kind of like I'd been slipped a note in gym class saying that there were red marks on the back of my shorts, and everyone was whispering and snickering behind their hands.

So Peek and me are going up the stairs, and the walls are bouncing, the stairs are bouncing. I'm in heaven. The bar is the first thing you see as you get to the top of the stairs, conveniently located for the extremely thirsty. Tyrone is mixing drinks for this woman with a purple mohawk and a spiked collar that looks like it could take someone's eye out. I catch his eye and he shouts, "Hey!"

"Been a while, Tyrone," PK says beside me and shakes Tyrone's wet hand.

"Yeah. Where the hell have you guys been?" The purple girl smiles and takes her drinks away but not before I recognize her.

"Hey Denise. Nice hair."

"Thanks, Magpie. Like yours too." We grin at each other. I hear Peek yelling over The Smiths about our finals.

"Final what?"

"Exams. For the year, you know?"

"Oh, good. So we'll be seeing more of you then."

"Yep. Absolutely. So how's the plight of the urban worker these days?"

"You know, I complain all the time but the Bolsheviks still haven't shown up. What're you drinking, same old thing?"

"Yep."

"How 'bout you, Mags?"

"Yep."

Tyrone, the Wednesday through Sunday manager and bartender, pours me what looks like a triple whisky and hands PK a brew.

He winks at us. "On the house," he says. "Congrats on

finishing." Peek and I grin at each other and stroll on over to the booths where hopefully some of our friends have already scored our usual.

It's a Thursday, which is sometimes a problem, being the international middle of the week drinking day. A lot of weirdos show up sometimes, thinking they can slink in and take over the joint and hand in their shitty music requests. Honestly, I don't even know why they bother, since there's a meathead bar just down the street especially designated for them. The upside to this is that the club always favours us above them and we usually end up pissing them off so much that they leave. There are always enough regulars to ensure our continued groove and safety.

Like a month before. I was dancing and some jock with this slick blond crewcut sidled up and tried to cop a feel on the dance floor. He just sort of waddled over and started acting like my shirt. So I backed up and got out of his way, thinking that maybe he was a crackhead or some shit, but he followed me around, pressing up to me. I started to say "back up, buddy," when all the sudden there was mass confusion. The dance floor sort of pulled together and gathered this guy up and carted him off the floor *en masse.* All these people that I'd seen before but didn't really know. A couple of guys hauled him over to the bar where Jackson arrived and escorted him outside. I haven't seen him since and, I've got to admit, I wouldn't like to know what's been done to him. But the funny thing was, no one missed a beat. They took him away and then went on dancing like nothing happened. When it was over I just stood there for a minute, I admit I was a little stunned, and this girl leaned in and said, "Hey, you okay? That guy was a real prick, eh?" I couldn't help smiling, and I started dancing, not knowing what to do with this funny feeling in my chest. Rule number one, like I said.

Belong to the club, and the club will belong to you.

It's something that pushes our buttons and turns us on. It's like we wear name tags that say: this is who I am, this is what I've been given, so fuck you. Our friends are the same. The disinherited, the underdeveloped, those unlucky enough to be born and raised in similar circumstances. We get to the booth and I take a look around and it hits home: Roddy's parents, for instance, are cokeheads. When Nathalie was five her mom bailed, stealing her little brother away, and she hasn't heard from them since. Derek lives with his mother, who entertains her 'boyfriends' for money. My brothers' best friend Zach has a father who likes to make cubist art out of his face and his mother died of cancer. And Benny? He'd been shuffled through about fifteen foster homes before we met him, and not one of them treated him as well as the average household dog. Alcoholic parents, glue-sniffing parents, people who beat and abuse, absent parents. Yeah, sure, everyone's got a sob story. Hell, my own family looks quite dainty in comparison. But you add that to the neighbourhood we live in and you end up with big, fat zeroes. The point is that everyone's got a story, and this is all translated somehow on the outside. It reminds me of the bikers hanging at the Bull, the way their Harley Davidson and Rebel flags wave off the motorcycles in the breeze. Something visible. Something that tells everyone where you belong. And that's where I like to stay—together, because it's easier than trying to force the world to let us in. It's better to stay in our clubs and on the streets where we rule things than go off and let others be the ones who bounce you.

PK is always telling me to be careful, not to romanticize the scene too much. We're going to get old, he says, and then where will we be? Like my mother, like his mother? Like one of those old biker chicks with her tits hanging out of her leather bra, all droopy with too many drugs and drunks? It's a really dangerous thing, he says, to take it too seriously. It makes you think that there are these walls that you can stay behind, where it's safe, but that only means you give up your courage to escape. He has a point, I'll admit. But I also know he feels the same way I do whenever we walk in and everyone is there, sitting in our regular booth. It kicks me with a kind of crazy happiness that tells me I'd better dance or I'll cry.

My brothers and Zach are sitting at the booth with our friends. Nathalie's out tonight, Derek drooling down her top beside her. Benny's already stretched out on the bench like a pimp. He's wearing this ridiculous hat that looks like he's going fishing, which just leads me to suspect that he wants to look like a pimp. Roddy, our resident primo dancer, is there with his dreads piled all around his face and dripping sweat. Zach is on the end, and I squish in beside him as my brothers start gaping at my hair.

They don't understand, my brothers. They look like identical poster boys for the Aryan youth club. Blond, light-eyed, freckled. The only thing that distinguishes them is that Joe's eyes are blue while Pete's are green. That and that Pete isn't nearly as buff as Joe, and Pete's the army pants type and Joe wears the leather biker pants in the family. Joe's also the one who inherited the filthy mouth from God knows where.

"What the fuck did you do!" he screams.

"Shut up, Joe. It looks good. For an Easter egg," Pete says.

Zach, their ever so much nicer friend, leans over and whispers into my ear, "I like it, Mags. It's cool. Suits your name." I smile my best vindicated female smile, but then he goes all serious and tells me, "If you tell your brothers I said that I'll have to kick your ass."

I belt him for good measure, and suddenly everyone at the

table starts yelling. Nathalie tells Joe and Pete to fuck off, Benny screams about drug market prices, Roddy tries to tell me I look great over the din. I mean, hey, it's only a little blue hair, right? PK just sits back and grins like a fucking dog. Hell, he has a right to, seeing as how he's the one who dyed it for me. He's still got the evidence all over his hands.

Zach Bennett might as well be another one of my brothers. He looks enough like them—another Aryan poster boy. Blond, eyes just a shade greener than Pete's. He's actually Pete's age, and really he's Pete's best friend, although the three of them are joined at the glass. People call him and Pete 'The Twins'.

Since we moved into our latest building Zach's been a fixture at our house. He's come over for dinner every other night since we were kids, and Fran never said a word. The nights he wasn't there were kind of quiet, dark. That was usually because Fran and Joe and Pete and I spent our evening wondering what colour Zach would be the next day, which parts would be rearranged, or if he'd even be breathing. Sometimes he came back looking just fine, and we would all breathe a sigh of relief that his old man passed out before doing some serious damage.

Other days Zach would walk in the door, sporting his newest shades of purple and blue and red, and sit down at the table all quiet and slow. Pete and Joe and I refer to Zach's dad as the Cubist, but we've never discussed him in front of Fran or Zach. He had to keep his dignity, after all. See, he'd sit down all beat up and then give a little laugh, more like a hiccup really, and he'd say, 'You should see the other guy.' He said the same thing every time. Fran would pull in her lower lip and suck hard, and just ladle out a huge glop of food onto Zach's plate—or as much as she could afford that week. "Let's fatten you up a bit, Zachary," she'd say, as if he didn't have a care in the world. But we all knew what she meant. And then Pete and Joe would start into the jokes, like, "Did you hear the one about the one-legged priest?" until pretty soon Zach was rolling peas onto the floor and just about pissing himself he was laughing so hard. We'd all heard them like a million zillion times, those stupid jokes, but we all still laughed. The other thing was that these were the only times my mother ever let a dirty word pass our table. It was the unspoken rule. Sometimes I even caught her smiling.

Like I said, Zach lived in the same building as us, only three floors above and on the other side. They moved here when Zach was eight, after his mother died, so I don't know what the hell he did before we showed up. All the same, every night that Zach wasn't over Fran spent a hell of a lot of time looking out the windows, craning her neck up to see if she could hear anything over the sound of traffic. Then she'd look down and try to peep around the corner to see if there were any ambulances or cops or some shit pulling up. In her own way, she was trying to protect him. There wasn't anything else to do. If we called child services he'd just be shipped out to foster homes, maybe end up someplace worse. And then he'd probably be returned to the Cubist, who'd surely kill him then. Besides, if he was taken away we couldn't keep our eyes on him. So Fran fed, and she watched. And we all held our tongues.

If there are any better times than when my brothers and Zach come out, I don't know what they are. I would be lying if I said that the slagging of my hair bothered me. Truth be told, I get off on it. I love my brothers getting all upset when I wear a slutty skirt or my hair's too colourful. I love that they hate it when I wear black eyeliner and black lipstick and black nail polish, so I do it all the more. Who wouldn't? So the table is in an uproar. Zach and Peek and I are all just smiling away at ourselves. The JD is kicking in, making my head swirl. I feel the beer and sweat-soaked vinyl of the bench underneath me. My palms spread against the seat, feeling its sticky, damp warmth. The music is so loud it beats into my hands, and under the lighting they look like sleek black cats. I look up and PK's gone, probably to the dance floor. Through a haze I hear Zach buzzing in my ear.

"Magpie? Earth to Mags. Get out of the way, already. There're people getting up."

"Uh, sorry," I say like a moron. Joe and Pete and Nathalie scuttle out, and Roddy, the little dancing demon that he is, is already out there.

"Are you okay?" Zach says. The JD is practically bouncing through me now, and I'm quite sure I've got the stupidest look on my face.

"Great," I sort of drool. "Never better."

"Y'wanna get up and boogie?"

"You know, you're a real corndog, Bennett."

I see the bobbing figures of my brothers on the crowded floor. The lights sparkle and churn, making it impossible to walk in a straight line. Somehow I'm always convinced that I'm tilted on an angle and I've got to wedge in with care. Zach propels me lightly from behind until we reach the others, but not before I step on the toe of a tall bearded man who kind of looks like a Deadhead castaway, who squeals and yells at me to watch it.

Pete's dancing kinda hunched over with a bottle in hand. Nathalie's pressing up to him from behind. Roddy's off somewhere in the centre of the fray, surrounded by hoards of admiring females. I close my eyes and cut loose. It seems like a long time before I open them again, and by this time I'm breathing hard from way too many cigarettes and my chest hurts with booze. Through blue strands of hair I look up and Zach's there, watching me while he dances. There's a funny little half smile on his face, so I think I'm drooling or some shit.

"What the hell's your problem," I say.

"Nothing. You're a good dancer."

"Hmm," I say, all self-conscious. I watch Roddy bounce up from the floor with a special hipster's twist and then head back to the table, Zach in tow behind me.

The drinks come fast and furious after that. Pete and Joe buy me a couple rounds, hoping to see their little sister turn green at the gills, no doubt. I'm on my sixth JD, toasting myself, "another JD for the DJ," when Spanky shows up, all sweet and shy. Derek spots him first, and I almost don't recognize him when Derek yells out and waves. He's walking around with his coat still on in the tropical heat of the club, his face hazy under the lights.

"Yo! Spanky. Spanky, you bastard!" He catches sight of us and comes over real slow, shrugs in front of the booth.

"I lost track of time," he says.

"C'mere, sit," Derek directs the traffic. "Nathalie, move your witch ass over."

"Don't talk to me like that." Nathalie looks into her glass as if she's bored. "Unless you're going to make it up to me later." She gives him this upward glance like she's a goth version of Rita Hayworth or something.

"Whatever, Ho," Derek grins at her. "Hey, this is Spanky. Spanky, everyone."

Spanky sits down on the edge of the bench. He's not exactly uncomfortable looking. More quiet. Like he's just hanging out, existing. Joe takes charge, gets Spanky a glass and fills him up.

"Here's to sex'n'drugs and rock'n'roll," he toasts. We all raise our glasses. Roddy's back on the dance floor. Nat is snorting into her rum and coke. I sit across from Spanky, watching him, and PK starts writing in the little book that he carries everywhere. Everything seems good, better than good. Time rushes into the room, into the now thinning room of our club. R.E.M. is singing about the end of the world, and we all belt out the lyrics as loud as we can. The DJ lowers the volume so we can hear ourselves. It's like we're all in it together.

Why I Hate Closets

I don't know what gets me thinking about it, if it's just a glitch in my memory or something else. I'm just lying on my bed, thinking over the night and it all sort of comes flooding back. Maybe it's because of Spanky. He's just so damned sweet and real that it scares me. I sat there in the club all night, watching him, trying to figure out where he fits in to the whole grand scheme of things. It might be that he gives me the vibe of a nice kid who could use some protection.

Anyway, once upon a time I had this friend, Jessica. We were friends a long time, Jessie and me. We did all those girly things together that PK would have ralphed at. She was also my one ticket into the lap of luxury. Her parents had plants that didn't die. There was an enclosed backyard with grass and a swing set, though we were too big for it. She had scads of books. She had double-length, glow-in-the-dark skipping ropes. She had two parents. Her family ate well and they had a TV that didn't come from a dumpster. There were no cardboard boxes anywhere in sight, no yellowing wallpaper and no bums sleeping in a lobby. When I look back I can say, sure, they were poor too. But at the time it sure looked like luxury.

Jessie and I went to all the sappy movies that PK refused to attend, listened to Madonna and Cyndi Lauper and Tears For Fears. Dancing, that's what I remember—around her bedroom, singing into her hairbrush. We played at being superstars, people from a better hood. Girls with a bright future. Jessie was also the first friend I ever had who didn't live in an apartment building. She lived in a townhouse, one of those 'we live on the left side and the neighbours on the right' deals. It was ugly and brown, but what it lacked on the outside it made up for on the inside. It was a classy dive.

I used to sleep over a lot. There wasn't really room for me at my place anyway. We lived in a really small apartment then, a two-bedroom. So I slept with my mom or my brothers, or on the floor, or on the fifteen-year-old couch. My mother was so tired I'm not even sure she noticed where I was sleeping.

The deal with Jessica was that she didn't have any brothers or sisters. She had a room of her own, which was, to say the least, exotic. Instead of siblings she had all these stuffed animals, piled fat stuffed sausages with glazed eyes. She made me sleep on the floor but I got over that pretty fast. The dinners at her house were real good and the television was in colour. I remember roast beef and Yorkshire pudding, the fluffy smell of potatoes with real butter. Fancy deserts like ice cream and brownies, homemade Nanaimo bars, cookies after school. It was my wet dream. And so I followed her around, feeling my hands hot and aching, and hoped no one felt sorry for me.

So I slept on the floor. No big deal—whatever she wanted. I'd never argue when she wanted to go to bed disgustingly early. I played with her hair, drew on her back with my fingertips. Anything. I would bunk down on the sleeping bag her father always pulled up from the basement for me, zip myself in and think about what it might be like to get new clothes for Christmas and birthdays.

Sometimes, during the night, I could hear Jessie's indrawn breath. It was like a broom sweeping across the floor, real slow. This would stop and be replaced by mumbling, her head tilting over to one side like she was listening to something. She'd sit up, eyes open, but I could tell she wasn't seeing me sitting there. Then there was this one time she slid her legs over the side of the bed and sort of stumbled over me to her closet. She always kept her closet door closed at night. I guess she'd seen *Poltergeist* one too many times or something. Anyway, she was afraid of her closet when she was awake. But when she was asleep it was a different story. She went over to the closet and opened the door. I whispered to her—"Jessie? You awake? Can you hear me, Jessie?" And she mumbled away: "Hmmh... Magpie. Don't bump your head on the way in." Then she closed the door behind her, and I heard her bedding down in the corner.

That first time my hackles went nuts. I didn't know what the hell she was talking about. So I got up and went over to the closet.

"Jessie, you okay?" It was the kind of closet door with the little slits in it, and I pulled at the accordion-style door. And there she was, curled up in a ball, eyes closed, hands tightly squeezed between her nightgown-clad legs. Sleeping.

I tried to whisper, but then I just talked out loud. "Jessie. Are you asleep? Are you dreaming? Are you gonna be okay? Do you want me to get your mom?"

Jessie's eyelashes flapped and opened. Her eyes looked like dark, fluttering moths. It was almost like she was awake, because she answered me very clearly.

"Don't call anyone. They can't fit in here. I think the closet's only big enough for us two. I need my teddy," she said, motioning like she was going to get up.

All I said was, "I'll get him for you, it's okay."

I walked over to her bed, where all of her animals slept beside her. I looked out the window, trying to see if she knew something that I didn't. I totally panicked. Even though it wasn't far from my place the street she lived on was quiet, empty. Only the rattle of the wind, only a newspaper floating past. I grabbed her favourite, a big stuffed animal named Hector from *The Bear Called Jeremy* show.

"Here's Hector, Jessie," I said. And she opened her arms for him, snuggled down with him.

"Quick," she said, her eyes shut tight again. "Get in

Maggie, and close the door."

And so I did. I closed the door on her. Only I didn't get in.

That first time I just slept on the floor all night, sort of not sleeping but watching the closet door, listening for anything that didn't sound right. The cracking of a bottle outside, the heavy footsteps of people coming home from the bars. Cars passing with a gentle roar, their headlights casting shadowy webs on the ceiling. But Jessie didn't budge. She slept as soundly and quietly as one of the stuffed animals that stared at me from the bed.

In the morning she came out looking fresh and well-rested. She pushed at the door, stood up and stretched. I'm not sure if she was ever even awake at that point. She acted as if nothing weird had happened at all.

After that first time, it happened every time I slept over. Every time. All things considered that was a lot of times. I took to sliding into her bed when she disappeared into her closet, experiencing what a real bed all to myself felt like. And each time it was the same: I'd go over, ask her if she was okay, hand her Hector. It got to the point that as soon as she made her move I'd have Hector in hand. It got to the point where I didn't even bother to sleep until she was going towards her closet filled with dresses that she was afraid of when she was awake, afraid to be outside of when she was asleep.

I tried to ask her about it. She'd pretend she didn't hear me or she didn't understand. "I do not sleepwalk, Maggie," she told me, and changed the subject or the record.

There was this time I saw her, after she'd moved, after things fell apart. Jessie was on a bus that was stalled at a red light and I was crossing the street. I put up my hand to wave at her, just held it up so that maybe she'd see me. Through the glass I saw her loose, dreamy eyes. Calm eyes, as though she was still asleep, dreaming her closet dreams. Empty eyes. Like I could finally read on her face what she'd been dreaming. Like I'd known it all the time.

Rule No. 3

We're the usual band of suspects at the club. There's a tingle at the back of my neck, maybe because of the bad dream I had last night. The booth is shifted one back tonight, not our usual, and I think of this as a bad omen. There's something bad everywhere, I think. My head is full of that rotten egg smell that rolls from the sewers.

Of course, everyone is having a ball. Peek and this guy with dreads are discussing politics. Derek is looking down the sleek black of Nathalie's dress. She's giggling back at him, doing this coy little shake. Roddy's out shaking his booty. Benny bounces in his seat. I swear to God he's actually vibrating, and he's going on about hallucinations and "good fucking drugs." Benny's totally fucking high is what he is. His audience is Spanky, who's become a regular member of our little troupe. PK pulls out his black book and starts scribbling away after Benny leans over and yells something in Peek's ear. I have a funny feeling this will be tonight's entertainment.

People come and sit with us every now and then. I forget to say hello to them. The room is a shade darker than I remember it. Under the ultraviolet lights my friends take on a sinister glow. Teeth are yellow instead of white. Benny is wearing his skeleton t-shirt. It's fucking with my head. My eyes feel like they're spinning out of their sockets.

I'm dirty. I haven't showered and my hair sticks up in thick blue tufts. I like it though, the sticky feeling on my skin, the slightly damp texture. When I touch my arm, my hand, it's hot and clammy. The dancers pound up and down on the floor and it's making me queasy. I can see the jiggle of the club. Everything is unstable. I imagine the floor boards caving in, people screaming as they fall through and lie in jangled heaps. Fuck.

I blink once and suddenly Joe and the Twins are standing in front of me. From behind there's this woman who puts her arms around Pete and Zach. They look vaguely amused. I'm completely disgusted to discover it's Cat. Her name is Caitlin, but she tells everyone to call her Cat. People let her hang because they're scared to tell her to go away. They're even more scared of letting her befriend them. I'm not afraid of either possibility tonight. I'm ready and willing to tell her to go to hell if she pisses me off. I'm in no mood.

Zach squeezes in beside me, putting his arm around my shoulder.

"What the fuck, man."

"Please, please protect me," he hisses. He's doing his best imitation of the intimate lean. His breath is a hot tickle on my neck and my brothers shoot him a weird look.

"What'sa matter, Bennett? Cat caught your tongue?"

"She's been following us since we got here."

"Nothing to be afraid of except a little VD, a few suicide attempts and some major league stalking."

"Meeow! Now don't be cruel, Smith."

"Well, are you just going to leave my poor brothers defenceless?"

"They have girlfriends. They can fend for themselves."

"Oh. Sure. Hey wait a minute. Pete doesn't have a girl-friend, does he?"

"Uhmm. I dunno. Wanna dance? I don't want to give her any opportunities." Cat, as we speak, is cozying in on the other side of the table. I feel her legs scrape up against Zach's, her weak "sorry." Then she doesn't move them.

"You owe me bigtime," I tell him. He takes my hand, making a big production out of it. On the dance floor he pretends that 'The Passenger' is a slow couples' song. I'm getting embarrassed and wondering what the hell.

We're turning ballroom style around the floor. People are starting to laugh, and as if on cue Zach starts mocking it up a bit. Then Nat and Derek start doing the same thing. He's dipping her all over the place and Nat's hair is smacking people in the kneecaps. Zach pulls the same thing. The down-to-the-floor dip makes me dizzy. Patches of red spread across his nose when he spins me upward. I don't know what possesses me but I touch his face, run my fingers under his left eye where there's still a scar. He winces.

"What," he says, all defensive.

"This time you're not all black and blue."

"What?"

"Last time we danced like this. 'Member?" I'm sorry I said it now. His face falls. Grabbing me closer he spins and spins me until I think I'm going to upchuck.

It's funny—Zach Bennett was the first boy I ever danced with. It was a long time ago, I think maybe I was 13 or 14. Fran had left for work hours before. Pete and Joe were at school and Zach was staying home with me that day. He'd spent the night on our couch after his dad started rearranging the furniture the hard way.

I handed him a cup of coffee and pushed his feet off the couch. It amazed me, then and now, how damned good-natured he was after a night of being pummelled into horsemeat.

He said, "So when are you gonna start coming out with us?"

"I guess when I'm old enough to pass." And then I thought about this and said, "Whenever Joe decides."

"He might just decide to keep you locked up forever. His sweet Catholic sister and all."

"Do I look sweet and innocent to you? Do I even *look* Catholic?"

"Lemme see." He lifted my chin, looked me all over, turning my head this way and that. I mean, he looked in my ears. He looked up my nose. And then finally he nodded, like he'd formulated the rest of my life. "Everywhere but the eyes."

"Well, I guess that's acceptable."

"How about me?"

"Definitely a little worse for wear."

"Yeah."

He collapsed back on the couch. His hair was standing on end and I remember I had this incredible urge to pat it down.

"You should comb your hair. You'll never pick up girls looking like that."

"What do I need to comb my hair for when I've got all these tough bruises." He tried to smile, wincing from the effort. I touched his bruises, ran my fingers lightly against his split lip, the oozing cut beneath his eye. The swelling was the worst there. He could barely open it, the skin all hot and puffy. His dad had really done a number on him. It wasn't the worst we'd seen, but it was bad enough.

"Good point," I said. "So you look like a bum with bruises."

"Ha ha." Zach jumped off the couch and went over to my mom's record player. He put on Fran's favorite record, *Sinatra's Hits, Volume One*, and cranked it. Horns blared through the walls. Zach did this little slow-moving Enrico Suave move.

"Don't tell me a bum like you knows how to dance."

"Sure I do." He held out a hand, bowed down as low as his sore muscles would allow. "Shall we?"

"You're kidding, right?"

"You gotta learn sometime, kid."

So I took his hand and he led me around the small table piled up with the breakfast dishes. Zach placed my hand on his shoulder, took my other hand. "Don't look at your feet," he told me.

"What the hell else am I supposed to look at? I don't know what I'm doing."

"Just follow my lead, and you've got to look at me. That's the way it's done."

"Yeah but you're ugly."

"Always charming, Magpie. Pretend I'm one of your pimple-faced idiot boyfriends."

"Quite the stretch." Then we were quiet. The livingroom swam behind his bottle-bruised face. He spun me and it was like I was in one of those Fred and Ginger movies that came on Sunday afternoons. The music filled up the room, got louder and louder. I couldn't believe Bennett could move like that. I literally had no idea. I thought I was going to fall when he dipped me. My hair hit the ground, and just when I felt my grip loosening—it was a long dip—he straightened me up, spun me again.

"Okay," he said and dropped my hands. "Dance lesson's over."

"Oh. Hey, that was kinda fun."

"Don't push your luck," he said. His face looked like it hurt him. He was breathing hard and his arms looked as if they were going to fall off.

"Did I hurt you?"

"Naw, I'm just tired," he said.

"Hey, where'd you learn those moves?" I asked.

"My mom. My mom taught me. Before she got sick." He turned off the record player, curled up again under the blanket and closed his good eye.

So we're not really dancing anymore, just shuffling around, and Zach's sort of staring through me at this point. I can't imagine what he's thinking, why he seems pissed at me. It wasn't good or anything back then, but we survived. I didn't mean to bring up the fact that he'd been recovering from another one of the really bad nights with the Cubist.

And then he finally goes, "Yep. I remember."

"Sorry. Didn't know it was a sore subject."

"Yeah well, it's hysterical how many things you don't know, squirt."

"Squirt. I don't think you've called me that in, like, three years."

"Well you're acting like one again."

"Typical older brother syndrome. Smart aleck."

"Luckily no relation," he says. I start walking away from him when he pulls me back onto the floor. "Wait a minute. You promised to protect me."

"I don't feel so good. I'm going home. Get Nathalie to do it. She'll do it for free if you look down her top."

"Gettin' awfully catty in your old age, Mags."

"Har Har, Bennett. Stuff it."

"I'll walk you home, okay? Then we'll both be protected."

"Whatever," I say. But secretly I'm glad because I'm starting to feel like shit. And then we get back to the booth and PK is pulling at my sleeve and making me sit down.

"Mags," he yells in my ear, "you gotta listen to this. This is great."

PK thinks a lot of things are great when he doesn't think everything sucks. I sit down, sighing, and I catch Zach's eye. He's looking extremely uncomfortable wedged in between Cat and Nat, the two wonder-boob sisters.

"What's up. I was just about to ditch—"

"Wait—wait—rules," he yells. Or that's all I catch, at any rate.

"I can't hear you, Peek."

"Me and Benzadrine came up with some great shit," he grins. "Club rules."

"Oh yeah? Why?"

Benny's laughing his head off in a pitcher of beer. Has everyone been passing around the crack pipe while I was up dancing?

"What do you mean 'why.' *Under*ground rules, Magpie."

"Okay, shoot," I say. "I'm listening. But make it quick, monkey boy."

"Drum roll please," Benny stands up and shouts as only he can. I swear about half the people in the club can hear it, even over the music. I think he's made me deaf. Pete and Joe at the booth behind ours turn around and start doing their best—and let me just say horribly bad—*rat a tat tat*. "Quiet, please. May I have some order in our house of ill repute. I now present our resident historian and lawmaker, PK! Ahhhh." He cups his hands and pretends to be a roaring audience.

"Thank you, thank you," PK bends low at the waist. I grab onto the table, thinking it can prevent my head from spinning. It doesn't work. "Today, ladies and gentlemen, we have before us an extraordinary task," PK says. I try to focus on his kinky curls and the wicked glint of his eyes beneath his glasses. "That of the rules of the club, etcetera etcetera. Are you ready?" His accent is laid on pretty thick. It's the Monty Python kind, all fake Brit and stuff. His tiny crowd cheers.

"Now, Benzedrine. Hand me the rules, please."

"Here you are, your foureyedness," Benny goes, and then bowls over laughing at how funny he thinks he is.

"Ahem. Rule Number One, of the Underground and otherwise aforesaid mentioned club—"

"Peek," Benny complains, leaning over PK's shoulder, "I can't read your writing."

"Doesn't matter. I know what it says."

"Go on, Peek," Pete yells. The tables crammed with regulars on either side of our booth are leaned over expectantly.

"Rule Number One. Drinking before three p.m. is highly appreciated."

There are some groans at this, some catcalls. The booth is throbbing. My arms and legs are starting to feel shaky, weak. The kind of feeling I hate the most.

"Rule Number Two. In order to be a productive and successful member of the club—i.e. initiate in drinking before three, until three—one must be a member of the club. Membership, after all, has its privileges." They're getting louder now, cheering. My head falls back and I can see the curious faces of some people I know, and the few, startled faces of those I don't. But they're all looking pretty damned amused.

"Rule Number Three."

"Louder, PK!" someone yells.

"Ahem." And now he stands up on the seat, steps up onto the table top while everyone moves their glasses out of the way. He scythes the air with one of his pale, bony hands towards the DJ's booth. The disco lights are slinking. Everything begins to sway. "Are you ready for Rule Number Three?"

"Yeah!" The table sloshes around on its greased axles and PK has to get a grip on his balance before he continues.

"Okay. Rule Number Three. Based upon Rule Number Two, proclaiming the simple but efficient credo that one must be a member and membership has it's privileges... blah blah blah... Don't fuck with the Regulars!"

Benny shoots up, screaming a Rebel yell. Everyone cheers, and the clink of glasses goes on for a while. It's better than the club singing happy birthday to some poor shmuck. I want to absorb it all but I've got this sinking feeling coming at me and it's knocking me under.

"Hey, Mags? Magpie?"

"Zach?" I do a checklist inside the blackout. I'm breathing. Check. I can feel my body. Well, most of it, check. Are you drunk? Naw. I've only had a couple of drinks. Check. How are your legs? I think I can walk, thanks for asking, Magpie. No problem, Magpie. Maybe you'll need some help, Magpie.

"Hey, are you alright? You want me to get you home now? You don't look so good."

"Zach," I say, and I pluck weakly at his shirt, "I've got to get out of here."

"C'mon," he says, grabbing my hand for the second time tonight. We slip out past the bar before the shouting dies down, before the end of the list.

"Wait here for a minute," Zach tells me. My head is now a bowling ball. He leaves me on the second flight down, before the final twist that leads out. And then he turns back and says, "I'm going to get a cab, okay? You're in rough shape."

"I'm not drunk, Bennett." My limbs, and especially my lips, feel blue. Numb.

"I know. That's what worries me."

"Do you think I could have been poisoned?"

"I dunno. It's probably just the flu," he tells me and strokes the hair off my forehead. "I'm going to get Jackson to take a look at you first."

"Jackson's got bad fucking breath," I say, and start to giggle. A bolt of pain knocks around inside my skull. "Don't you think it's ironic," my tongue wags to Zach as he recedes, "that the club is named the Underground but really it's on the second floor?"

"Just don't move for a sec, okay."

"Sure. I'll pretend I'm on vacation. In Tahiti." I can tell he's worried, looking at me intently as I slump down against the wall, onto the stairs that have definitely seen way too much vomit and beer slick. There's more banging downstairs.

People are yelling. I think down is up and up is down. Aren't the people yelling upstairs? Could I get back into the club by going downstairs for once? My fingers slide against the sweating wall as I crawl my way, half crouching. The banging is getting louder. It sounds like a hockey game. PK's rules, I think. Everybody loves them. The last corner slides beneath my fingers. Only one more flight of stairs. Zach's hair is a halo of gold under the lights of the stairwell. He's standing stock still on the fifth stair. I have to stand up to see beyond him.

"This wasn't in the brochure," I say. My stomach heaves.

It's the door. I think I'm hallucinating. I take a hand and check the heat bursting off my forehead.

"I've got a fever," I hear myself mumbling. My teeth chatter loudly in my skull. "I'm seeing shit."

The door looks as though it has been rained on by big, shiny, cupid-red crayons. There are patterned drops on the steps, under my feet. I follow them carefully until I'm on the step just above Zach. There's shouting outside. It's the rules of the club all right, but I'm sure it's not quite what PK had in mind.

"Magpie, get upstairs and stay there. I'll come and get you at the bar."

"What the fuck's going on," my teeth chatter, and I sink down onto a step. I can see Jackson's arm pulling a vice on some guy's neck. With the other he pounds the face into the glass of the door. But it's not really a face any more. Crack. Once more. The glass snaps and crackles—or maybe it's the guy. Two other members of the club are standing around, and as Jackson lets the guy slide onto the ground they pick up the slack, pumping him with their legs. Into the ribs, the head, the legs. I can hear them shouting: *You're lucky we ain't packing pipes, you stupid fuck. You're lucky we don't carry guns, you piece of shit. You're gonna wish you were never born, motherfucker. What, you're not gonna cry for your mama? Shut the fuck up, you fucking faggot.*

That stupid voice inside my head is going off and telling me stupider things. Like, he's not a faggot. You guys don't beat the shit out of fags here unless they pay you to. Like, a faggot is a bundle of sticks.

His hand goes up, the guy's. The bloody piece of pulp's hand goes up. It's all red. Everything is red except the darkness of the hallway and the yellow light off of Zach's hair. "What the fuck is going on," I ask again. I can't stand up. I can't feel my legs. The guy enacts a full body shiver when Jackson's steel-toed foot careens into his ribs. And then Jackson's smoky voice echoes through the glass: *Don't kick him too hard in the head.* But the guy, he doesn't even raise his arms over his head. He doesn't even protect himself. Put your hands up, man, my head is trying to tell him. He must be too far gone. My stomach flips over again.

"Magpie, I told you to go back upstairs."

"Zach I'm sick, right? This is all a big hallucination." I'm not looking at him. I'm looking at the pulp on the sidewalk. No one even stops to watch except the hot dog vendor who parks outside the door and he's packing up his stuff as if his life depends on it. It's just us, staring. When I finally look at Zach I know he's freaking. His face is drawn tightly across his cheekbones, and he's got a slash of scarlet across his nose. That always happens when he's upset.

"For Christ's sake, Magpie."

"Don't tell me what to do." I shake his hand off my arm. I can't stand up. The stairwell spins under my butt. My head is floating on the ceiling. I'm looking down on the two of us, on the stairs. I'm looking over the body of the man on the sidewalk, who definitely will not be able to walk. The beating is slowing down. Jackson gives the guy a final solid 'thwack' with his toe. This guy who is suddenly transformed, no longer human looking. His face resembles a garbage dumpster, a runny mass of broken eggs and orange juice. Even his eyes are bleeding tears.

I look up at Zach again. "Could you help me up?" It looks like he's thinking about it a little too long for my liking. "Please?"

"Maybe we should go out the back way," he pulls me to my feet and I totter a little. I can feel a slipperiness. There is red on the soles of my boots, I know. I hear Zach talking and the noise is red, like something backfiring through fog.

"Shhh, shh," I say. "We can't get out. We'll have to wait."

"But the back way, Mags. The fire escape."

"I can't do the stairs, Zach. Fuck." A sea of spittle forms beside the body that's lying prostrate in blood puddles. My stomach picks itself up. A step, and then another. And I can hear myself thinking from far away, like a telephone conversation that I'm overhearing: is this what it's all about? All our fine club rules that protect us? The person on the other end of the line sounds shocked and appalled. "You should see the other guy," I say to the door.

"C'mon." Zach opens the door gingerly, his fingers testing it as though it will scrape and wake up the neighbours. I dig into Zach's neck, my arm thrown over his shoulder like a feather boa.

"If my boots get ruined," I whisper, "I'm gonna kill some-one." My reflection is in the red glass, winking at me off the dark backs of the men outside. Blue hair winks, a startlingly white face winks. I don't recognize the eyes. They look like saucers full of milk.

"I don't know what we should do," Zach says. "No back door, and the cops are on their way, no doubt. I think that guy's just about had it."

"Great, Bennett." I grit my teeth and my jaw feels as though it's been welded together. "We'll just have to step over, then."

"Fucking asshole." It's Stevie. Fucking Stevie. Resident worm and tough guy. His bright orange hair is on fire. "Fucking asshole. Think's he can get away with shit like that here." Stevie poises his boot like he's getting ready to kick a soccer ball instead of this poor-ass guy. Only when it connects it makes the sound the ball makes when half the air is gone.

"Jackson." The words come out like the mew of a drowning kitten, I'm embarrassed to say. So much for my tough gal routine. He's got a full lurid grimace thing going on over his features. He's wiping sweat off his chin and forehead with the back of a dirty fist. His eyes look strange, relaxed. Not even a bit upset. Zach hoists me up further, holding my arm.

"What happened to you, Magpie?" Jackson asks, turning to look me over. His eyes. They're terrible. "Have your brothers seen you?" I am a gaping fish mouthing words. The street holds the sweet tinge of iron. I run the taste around my tongue.

"She's sick, not drunk, man," Zach defends me. Jackson sticks that same fist on my forehead and I cringe. My eyes close against the red and the earth spins quicker.

"Holy shit, Zach. Maybe you should wait for the ambulance and take her with this guy," he points down at the ground.

"No! Don't you fuckin' dare."

"It's okay. Shh. He's joking, Mags."

I see Jackson's eyes glittering, passing a look from me to Zach. He was not kidding.

"What-the-fuck, Jackson. What—the—fuck—" I sputter, a

raving lunatic now.

Stevie opens his big fucking mouth and crows. He's so fucking proud. "He fucked with the bull and he got the horns, man. You don't fuck with us, you know what I mean?"

I open my eyes, unable to believe I'm hearing such corny, stupid shit. "Shut your trap, you stupid piece of shit."

"Who do you think you're talking to, bitch? You want me to do that to you?" Stevie is foaming at the mouth, spittle flying with every round syllable. "I should take you down a peg or two, you fucking ho?" He actually starts fiddling with his belt buckle. He's got to be out of his frigging mind.

I can feel Jackson, more than see him, reaching out and grabbing Stevie by the neck and hoisting him into the air for a minute before setting him down, away from me. Sirens begin to wail from somewhere—on the streets, beyond the buildings across from the club. Or maybe from behind.

"If you ever," Jackson whispers to Stevie's purple face, "and I mean ever, say another word to Magpie that is not respectful and nice, I will personally decide your fate. I will have your house burnt down. I will have your mother beaten with pipes. And I will have your balls severed from your body with rusty razor blades. Do you understand this or do you need some encouragement?" He shakes Stevie's neck before it slides out from between his fingers.

Stevie rubs. There are livid red marks in the shape of thick fingers across his throat. "Yeah man, fuckin' chill, okay? I was just fuckin' around."

"You're getting too uppity, Stevie. And if you fuck with this girl, you will die. You don't fuck with my club, Stevie," and he sounds serious. "If you haven't learned that yet tonight, then maybe you ought to find another venue."

"Yeah, yeah, man," Stevie mumbles. "I'm going inside to find me a joint. You comin', Bruce?"

"In a while. I'm waiting for the cops." Bruce is the quiet one, Jackson's shadow. He follows Jackson around, study-ing—or at least this is the way it looks to me—his peace, his purpose. He doesn't look the type to beat people up, or to bounce. He's got the tall, skinny build of his Ukranian back-ground. Dark hair, the whiter than white skin. But he's mas-tered Jackson's eyes and movements. Economical, serene, and fucking crazy.

I wince as Jackson feels my forehead again. "Wait a sec-ond, Stevie," he says, and in a flash his hand goes from my face to Stevie's arm. "Don't you have something to say to the lady?"

Stevie's eyes flash pure hatred. "Yeah. Guess I do. I forgot," he says sarcastically. I'd personally love to slap him silly. "Pardon my rudeness, Magpie. Didn't mean to *frighten* you." Jackson's hand tightens, and I can tell he's hurting Stevie. "Sorry, okay?" he mumbles, and Jackson releases him so quick it throws Stevie off balance.

"Take her to the doctor tomorrow at least," Jackson says to Zach without skipping a beat. I try to rub red marks off my forehead. Can't everyone see us? I start to wonder. Maybe we're invisible. Maybe we are the only ones who can see all this.

"What happened, man?" Zach tries real hard to bring his voice down, make it sound conversational. Jackson leans against the shell of the club, the dirty brick. Folds his arms in front of him.

"This piece of shit broke on up to the DJ booth, filled his bag with all of Jeremy's music and shit while he was taking a leak. Jeremy caught him trying to unload all the equipment and shit, too." And even in my sick-as-a-dog haze I think to myself, that's it? That's all the poor bastard's done?

"A crate of records. The fucking microphone, man. And Jeremy ain't insured, eh? Supposedly this guy has been around to other clubs, too. I heard from Jake down at the Haze that they been ripped off real bad. They think it was this guy."

"Jeez, was he ever stupid," Zach says.

"Somebody better come quickly," Bruce breaks in, studying the arm of his leather jacket. It's like a science project. He's poring over his jacket analyzing the amount of blood per the man's condition. "He's a bleeder."

"So this guy's gonna fucking die over some records," I hear myself say out loud.

"Yeah," Jackson says, all quiet and still now. "So I fucking kill him. No one steals shit from my club."

Zach takes my arm and leads me away from the scene. There's a high-pitched squeal coming from somewhere, but I can't tell if it's in my head or the cops on their way. Bits of this guy's teeth are scattered like hen feed on the sidewalk. Pointing every which way is his red tattoo that will be there tomorrow, a fan or an anchor branching out and leading us in the doors. I can see our footprints like dark rain behind us, slick and glistening. My stomach gives another rise and I dry heave off to the right. The gagging is a suffocation. I pant. I retch emptiness. Zach stops to help me, holds me up.

"There's nothing in there," I tell him.

"It's okay," he says.

"Our footsteps," I say. He looks back then, the fluted patterns ending at our present position, like we've been dancing again. "Everyone can see, see? It's the indelible mark."

"Magpie, shh. You're sick."

"Don't fuck with the club." I'm trying to laugh but it comes out with a rough edge on it that I almost don't recognize.

"Yeah. Yeah, I hear you."

"Zach?" He struggles with my weight for a minute. I've been slumping against him.

"Move your legs, Mags. Gotta get you home."

"I don't want to be here any more. I don't want people to know that I saw that. It's in the eyes, you know. You know?"

"Uh huh. Shh."

Sleeping Dogs Lie

"It's sort of like I've stepped through a mirror," Zach tells me.

I'm propped up against my door, and he's searching through my little sack like a demon.

"What the hell are you talking about, Bennett." I feel drunk. Colours fade and wheel in front of my eyes. The door that separates me from my apartment, my bed, is closed, locked. Maybe even double-locked.

"It's not often," he says, pausing over a tampon, "that I'm the one just watching the crap being beaten out of someone. Usually I'm the one on the receiving end." He picks up the tampon, tosses it on the ugly carpet of the hall. "It's just plain weird. A parallel universe."

I try to imagine that mirror, what it looks like through Zach's eyes. And then I think of my apartment door as the same kind of mirror. My hand rests on the wood, my face presses up against it and I inhale toxic paint smells and grime. For some reason I'm thinking of my mother lying in her bed, dreaming of her long-gone husband or the priest who keeps her company every now and then. I picture her dreaming all Tetris-style of cleaning the steps to the altar every Saturday, bending down on hands and knees. I imagine this voice in her dreams, telling her there's no escape. She cleans the windows, her hands baked in chemical juices and stained glass light. Scrubbing the quaint bathrooms of the old Cathedral. A perfect toilet bowl gleaming like a new set of teeth. "It's not like she has a choice," I tell the door. I don't know why I'm thinking about this like it's a stunning revelation or something. But all the sudden I'm bowled over by it, how sad it is that my mother didn't have any choices. Then I'm sad for me—because suddenly I want some choices in life too. And I don't know where to get them.

"I'm not going in," I say to Zach.

"What're you going to do, Magpie?" He looks exasperated. "You're sick. Where the hell's your key?"

"I dunno. I think maybe I gave 'em to PK. To put in his pocket. I was supposed to stay at his place tonight."

"Jesus H. on a Pogo stick, Mags. What the hell were you thinking?"

"Watch your mouth, young man," I tell him, and push myself away from the door. "I was s'posed to be dancing. You see any pockets on this skirt? You think it would have been wiser to leave my keys in my bag for any asshole to grab? Take me to PK's then."

"Naw. We barely made it here. I gotta get you some aspirin or something. You're burning up."

"I'll sleep on a park bench. I don't care. I'm too hot anyways." I pluck at my t-shirt like it's a hot summer's sun beating down instead of flourescent hall lighting.

"Why don't we just get your mom up? Ring the doorbell."

I level a look at him, or as far as I'm capable of at the moment.

"Zachary Bennett. Do you really want to be the one responsible for getting my poor, hardworking mother out of bed?"

He pauses, his face tilted up like he's seriously pondering this.

"No," he admits. "Well, come on then."

All the colours have gone soft now, soft and exotic. It's a hazy screen slipped over everything. Zach walks me back to the elevator, curses after a few seconds of waiting.

"Just hold on, okay? Just don't pass out or anything."

A quiet 'beeng' of the doors, the mechanical sliding motion, and the elevator opens. Newspapers and flyers scatter to the corners of the rubber floor. Is it rubber?

"Are we going to the park?"

"Shh. No. Stop being such a crackhead."

"Ha ha. You crack me up." My head lolls back on my neck and I feel about a hundred years old. "No really. Where are you taking me? I think I have a right to know." Zach presses a button on the panel. The door clumsily shuts and bangs, and we fling upward. "Ah, man, this elevator's making me feel sick."

"It'll only take a second. Just hold on." We walk out on a higher floor. He leads me around the corner, and then down the hallway to the back side of the building.

"Hey, are you taking me to see the Super, Zach? Or—wait—are we going to *your* place?"

"Yeah. Just be quiet, alright? Don't wake up the building."

"I've never been to your place."

"No big shocker there, Magpie. No one has except Joe and Pete." He lets go of me while he fetches his keys from his pocket, fiddles with the locks. I slump myself against the wall. It's cinderblock. Like downstairs. Ugly cream painted bricks. Meant to sap the will right out of you. The door opens and he switches on the lights.

The livingroom and kitchen are sparse, shabby. Marks dot the walls and doors. A pile of dishes and beer bottles hide the counter. It looks worse than PK's dive.

"Holy shit," I say, unable to stop myself. "No wonder no one ever comes here."

"Shut up, Magpie."

"Is your dad here, because if he is I'm not—"

"He's not here. Don't worry. He's got a new girlfriend."

"Oh. I didn't know that."

"Well, there's no reason why you should. It won't last long, anyhow. It never does."

"He's such a bastard."

"Come on. This way to my room."

A door opens to the left of the very bare hallway. I can see his father's bedroom door open down at the end.

"Are you sure your old man isn't going to come back or wake up and decide to kick both our asses?"

"He won't—he just got his pogey check today. Besides, if he does, don't worry. He won't lay a finger on you." Zach turns his bedroom light on and the room blurs with patches of black and blue and white. His room—so ironic. The perfect colours for a bruise.

"I wasn't worried about my own fingers." I sink onto the blue-covered bed. The walls are thickly plastered with posters of *Sid and Nancy*, *Taxi Driver*, *Raging Bull*.

"Didn't know you were such a movie buff, Zach." He sits down of the bed beside me, bends down, begins unlacing my boots. "Pardon me," I cock an eyebrow at him, "but what the hell do you think you're doing?"

"You have to go to bed, Mags. And you ain't putting those clodstompers anywhere near my friggin' bed."

"I can do it myself."

"Oh, and I bet you can sing the national anthem standing on your head and juggling fire, too, but for right now let me feel like the tough guy, okay?"

He's quiet for a while, and so am I, trying to come up with a really good comeback. But when I lie back on my elbows while he's trying to figure out my steal-proof knot system, I realize that witty comebacks aside, I'm not even sure I can undress myself, let alone take the time to unlace my own boots. "Why is the room still spinning," I say. Zach's shirt pulls up from his waist as he works. I'm face to face with a long, jagged scar on the patch of skin beside his tailbone. "Do you ever wonder why people like to fuck other people up," I blurt out. I start to really regret it for a few minutes, while he keeps unlacing me, the first boot landing with a kerplunk.

"When I was a kid," he says, sitting up, "when my mom

was still alive, I never really thought about stuff like that. Sure, my dad had a temper, but life was pretty peachy. But then she got so sick. She used to cry. No—it was more like screaming. You couldn't even touch her skin. I tried to hug her and she'd scream. I thought it was me, that I'd hurt her. I didn't know we couldn't afford enough painkillers to keep her sane. She went crazy, eh. From the pain. And then she died, and I swear to God I thought it was 'cause I touched her."

"Everyone thinks that when they're kids."

"Yeah, you're right," he says. And then he goes, "But then my dad started turning into the asshole monster around that time. I guess he thought it was my fault too. So when he started goin' nuts on my ass, he would tell me I deserved it. And I believed him. I thought everyone deserved to really fucking hurt. 'Specially me."

"You were a stupid kid, Zach."

He smiles a bit, which is what I wanted him to do. "I think it was the day that Pete got hit by that car and got his wrist broken that I thought maybe it wasn't supposed to be that way. You remember that? Sixth grade. I mean, why should Pete suffer? Just because he's walking across the street with me? He'd done nothing wrong that I knew of, you know? Your whole family—you guys took me in. And all you do is suffer too. And I hate it. And I started to think, there's no reason for any of this. There's just nothing to it. We don't all deserve it. Shit just happens."

That sort of pisses me off, so I go, "Was that just 'shit happening' tonight? Was that random too?"

Zach doesn't say anything. He finishes untying my other boot, pulls it off along with my sock. I lose sight of him for a moment when he disappears with my boots, but then he's back, handing me a t-shirt and boxer shorts.

"I'll be back in exactly five minutes, Magpie. Don't you

fucking pass out half-dressed, y'hear me?"

"Yes master," I mutter and try to give him an obscene wink. My hands fumble as I try to pull them on. And then he's back, and the room's turned into molasses. He pulls the cover down, slides me in. Forces a couple pills down my throat. I feel something cold on my forehead, pressing. It's a cloth that feels soft, like my mother's fingers a million years ago, and the room goes black.

It hits me when I wake up in the tiny bed, Zach beside me, that I dreamt of them again. Blue sunlight streams through the curtains. Blue curtains that remind me of the candles at the church, sunlight off a wick in a blue jar. I know what I'll see if I open those curtains. Unrelenting gray. Masses of concrete and laundry floating off of balconies washed out by the light. Sequined buildings dressed in stucco and cement. Cracks on the sidewalks, weeds growing through and up, so far below the building. On either side of this one was another, and another, and another apartment building, and beside them stores tucked into the wrinkles. I don't want to see outside. I don't want to go outside.

My head is pounding like The Village People are throwing a party, and my face is wet. Did I bawl like a baby in my sleep? I feel a nervous itch running from head to toe. I slide a hand down my stomach. My body feels like it's melting. There's only hot flesh, burning crawling flesh. That's what it's like, I guess. Intentionally or not people leave their scars on you. One night you go to sleep and you remember too much. You wake up and there it is again. Fresh internal bleeding. There they were, in my dreams. Three little girls. Samantha Smith, Jessie. Me. And there's nothing I can do to save us.

"Magpie, you 'wake?"

"Yeah," I whisper back, and wipe my face.

"How d'you feel?"

"Really bad, Zach. Really bad."

"Are you going to throw up?" Zach sounds more awake suddenly. He sits up beside me. Heat burns off his body in a thick shroud.

"No. But I need to go home."

"Oh," he says, and I think he sounds vaguely disappointed. "What time is it?"

"You're asking me?"

"No, I guess not. I should've known better." I finally get the courage to look over at him. His hair is sticking up. I watch him rub his eyes, look around for his clock.

"Hey," I say, struggling to sit up, "I didn't know your dad was on the dole."

"Six months now. No—wait. I think it's up to eight now. He got fired from the trucking company."

"Same ole' same ole'?"

"Yep. Went to work drunk out of his tree again. Thought they wouldn't notice. At least they were nice about it this time. They pretended to lay him off."

"How do you know they didn't?"

"Just do. Come on, Mags. You've never even met the man. I've had the bad fortune of having to put up with him forever."

"Good point. Where are my clothes?"

"Just a second." Zach tumbles out of bed and lurches towards his closet, grinning shyly.

"Aw, look. They're even folded. What a prince you are."

"Shucks, miss, it weren't nothin' much."

"No, I mean it, Zach. Thanks for looking after me last night. I know it probably wasn't my finest hour. I mean, I owe you one."

"Hey, I don't need you to thank me." I occurs to me that his face isn't turning red out of embarrassment. I think he's mad. "I'm not kidding around, Mags. You and your mom and Pete and Joe. You guys saved my life. Don't you get it?"

"Well you don't have to go getting all snippy about it."

"I'm not getting—"

"And for another thing. I don't want your bloody gratitude any more than you want mine. Okay? I had nothing to do with so-called 'saving' you. If you want to display gratitude, go thank Fran and buy her a year's worth of groceries, which is about what you owe her. Okay? And other than that, you're fucking family, alright?"

He laughs. He bloody laughs. I can't help it. I start laughing, too, until we're both practically rolling on the floor. Snot threatens to spray the room—that kind of laughing. And then I stop, because I still want to throw up. But I also figure we're both kind of hysterical and far too undressed for my liking. And there's a thing in my brain that tells me something awful happened but my mind refuses to see it. No flash replays or anything. When I look down that avenue all I can see is bloody footprints strewn with teeth leading away from the club. I run to the bathroom holding a hand over my mouth, like something in the movies.

Her eyes are all red and panicky when I knock on the door. "Mary Margaret Smith, where the hell have you been? PK telephoned over this morning looking for you and where the hell were you, girl?"

"Fran, chill." I look like hell, I know, and I know this scares the shit out of her. My hair is sticking straight up in blue knots. My face is a bunch of red blotches and ultra pale in all the unred spaces. If she had any real information about this neighbourhood she'd be asking me if I've said no to drugs recently.

"Don't you talk to me that way, Mary Margaret. You're not

too old that I can't wash your mouth out with a good dose of Lysol."

"Mom, I'm sick. That's it. Stomach flu or something. I couldn't get home by myself and so Zach took me, but when we got here I was too sick to be alone and I'd given my keys to PK and I didn't want to wake you." I take a deep breath here, feeling kind of dizzy from the speech. "Don't worry," I say, watching this information sink in, "he wasn't home."

"Who wasn't home? Zachary?"

"Naw, Fran. Mr. Bennett. That's what you were thinking, right?"

"Shut your trap and come over here and sit down," she says, straightening her shirt and bustling over to the cupboard to check her medical supplies. I sit at the chair she's motioned to, taking in her grub clothes. Sweat pants that show how her stomach rounds, where she once carried us all.

"What are you doing home, Mom?"

"You're a stupid girl, Mary Margaret. Do you really think I could go to work when I didn't know where you were? When you could be lying dead somewheres?" She puts a cool hand to my forehead, pulls the old lemon face and makes her little tsk tsk noises, as if my getting sick wasn't by accident. "You're very warm," she finally says.

"Yeah, I know. And I would have come down sooner but I had a date with the Bennetts' toilet bowl."

She scowls at me again. "You were drunk."

"Naw, I wasn't even drinking," I tell her. The smell of booze is on me, though, and cigarette smoke, and if I concentrate hard enough I can probably make out the faint tender scent of dried blood. "Fran, I think I want to go to bed now. Please."

"Take a hot bath first. Not too hot, mind you. It's not good for you. And wash that filthy mess of hair while you're at it."

"Okay, Mom."

"I'll bring you in some aspirins in a few minutes. Try to keep them down as long as you can, hear me?" I hear it in her voice. She almost sounds positively chipper. And it's not just because she gets to miss a day of work on account of me. She always sounds that way when I get sick. I think it's her mother instinct, but it's probably more about our neighbourhood. Fran gets to be happy because she's sure of where I am. Her big eyes get to stay trained on me, and she knows, at least for today, that I'm safe.

So I do what Fran says. I take a bath in the tub that's been bleached by my mother's hands into a fine powdery blue. I strip off my clothes and I'm suddenly freezing, even though it's probably about a gazillion degrees in the apartment. I'm thinking about calling PK. I mean, I don't want him to worry about me and all. But for the first time in I think my life I don't know what to say to him. It's not just that some guy had the stuffing beaten out of him—it's more like my own head's been cracked open. Like the insides of my head is the top of a soft-boiled egg that once you crack, you can't stop the yolk from oozing out all around you.

Of course, I know what PK would say. He'd say something sarcastic and silly like, "Primitive rage, Magpie. Cro-Magnon man rears its ugly head." Or: "Survival of the fittest—you just gotta duck until they finish killing each other off." I don't want to hear PK's cute remarks.

The water is boiling hot but I'm still cold. Thighs quivering under the water, fists curled tight against my chest. I feel like I've been beating myself up. And then my mind is tripping around, wondering what would have happened if Jackson hadn't been there to stop Stevie the worm. Truth is—and here's PK's voice pealing through my brain again like he's the captain of the second coming—there's no guarantee. No matter which side you belong to. Even the presidents and millionaires die. You can die in a plane crash. You can be hit by a car just as easily as by a fist. Your house could burn down. There could be a nuclear war, and your city might not be directly hit, but there's always nuclear fallout, nuclear winter, poisoned water supplies that stretch from the States directly to here. And I'm getting in a little too deep even for me, and I'm thinking to PK, *can't there be some fucking thing that doesn't hurt to think about? Isn't there something we can do about all this?* "Go dancing," the Peekster in my head says, with that funny little half smile of his that only shows the teeth on the right side of his face. I feel his hands across my arms, and there they burn with cold. Sweat. I start to sweat buckets and I want to call Fran in. You can put me to bed today, Franny, I want to whine. I'll even let you comb my hair.

The room buzzes, or maybe it's only my ears. I can hear voices coming from the kitchen. The clock tells me it's ten-thirty. I've been out of it all day.

They're playing poker around the kitchen table. Beer bottles and rum clutter the spaces between the cards and the pot. And I'm so surprised that they're playing with real money I forget that I'm only wearing boxers and a tee. I mean, Zach may be family but I don't necessarily feel comfortable running around in my skivvies in front of him. "Well, look who's up," Joe mouths off. He's barely looking at me, though. He's busy pouring himself a rum and rum—hold the ice, hold the mix, hold the water.

"How are you feeling," Zach smiles at me.

"Better. I'm not going to die. Yet."

Pete goes, "Hey Mags, you comin' out tonight?"

"What, are you on crack?"

"Don't be an asshole," Zach punches him in the arm.

"Getting awful defensive of my sister there, Bennett."

"Yeah, well if I didn't who would, ya filthy whoremonger."

"Shut up the both of you," Joe grits through his teeth. "Fran's sleeping and I'd like to keep it that way. And I wouldn't want to be in your shoes if you wake the dragon lady from her slumber."

I walk over to the fridge, pour myself the last of the apple juice. I decide to sit down for a minute as far away from Zach as I can manage and try to appear unfazed. Zach puts his hand down one card at a time, and without looking at me asks, "Did you go to the clinic today?"

"Nah," I grin at him, "did you?"

"I'm not the one who was sick as a dog yesterday."

"By the way, my dear little sister," Joe levels some serious eyes on me, "you should have fucking told us. We would have taken you home."

"Ah, but you see, my friends, it was all part of an elaborate scheme to keep Cat away from me."

"Yeah. I mean, as Zach put it so well yesterday, at least you two have girlfriends to keep her at bay. Poor Zach here has no one."

Pete goes, "What happened to Sarah?" I suddenly feel my face go as hot as Zach's looks.

"Sarah who?" I frown. "Sarah the blonde who wears the leather pants and *thinks* she can dance?"

Pete looks annoyed. "That's the one."

"Yuck," I pull a face. "For crying out fucking loud, Bennett. I thought you had better taste than that."

"She's hot and you know it," Pete says.

"She's a fucking dog."

And now Zach is really starting to sweat. "Well, I didn't ask your opinion now, did I."

"Well maybe if you did you would have known better."

"What, are you a jealous girlfriend suddenly?" Pete's kind

of snickering like he thinks this is the funniest thing he's ever thought of.

"We weren't dating or anything, alright? We hung out for like a week."

Before I know it I'm shooting off my mouth as only I know how. "Way to be a stand-up guy, Zach. That's some real respect I see. You can't even admit you were—"

"Why don't you just settle down and keep your mouth shut?"

"Don't you go agro on me, Bennett. I've known you since you were practically in diapers."

"Uh, hello. But I think it's the other way around."

"Well, pardon my French but—"

"Time, time. Hey, time the fuck out." This is Joe, who crosses his hands ref-style. "Shut up the both of you. Mags, you're sick. Go to bed. Now."

"What the hell's your problem," I scowl, doing my best tough guy in front of the biggest brother impression. "I live here, y'know? I can practically vote."

"Mags," Joe sighs. I can tell he's quickly losing patience.

"Well, I can tell when I'm out of style. Goodnight one and all," I say, making a grotesque exit as graceful as I can. Everything's starting to seem like a bad re-run of *The Twilight Zone*.

Cucarachas

The other night is ringing in my head like someone tripping the fire alarm during exams. And it's not just what happened at the club—it's that frigging nightmare that gets my guts twisted into pretzels. But now it's all mixed up with what happened—the guy's teeth all over the sidewalk, Stevie pulling a fast one. So while I'm lying here it just plays over and over, like one of those instant replay things when you're watching hockey. And then, out of nowhere, I hear Fran doing voice over as the scene plays again: *Keep your eyes peeled, Mary Margaret.* Personally I don't think it matters what you see. Seeing doesn't make a lick of difference. It keeps coming anyway. And I wish it would disappear, all the red washing out of my head. I'm being a baby, I know that. But it feels pretty familiar: this is how I used to feel, when I was a kid. Abso-fucking-lutely hopeless.

When I was a kid the main topic of conversation at school was World War III. It came up during lulls in music class and assemblies. It went along the rows of kids, lip to lip, ear to ear, like a game of broken telephone. We passed doomsday to each other while playing frozen tag at recess.

It got a little out of control, I guess, because after a while I couldn't sleep at night. I was constantly shocked that people could know there wasn't any hope. But they still got out of bed in the mornings. They still brushed their teeth, ate their Cheerios, straightened their ties. Fran still cleaned the church even though there obviously was no God.

So we all kind of walked around wondering what was coming next, if there would be a next. And then Jessie had this great idea. She was going to write to the leaders of all of the major countries and tell them why they needed to put an end to all sorts of crap. Nuclear bombs, the Cold War that felt like a permanent chill. The Star Wars project.

Maybe I worried about it so much because it seemed more

out of control than some dude knocking your head in for a pint of beer or a bottle of Listerine, or raping you in the parking lot. I mean, you could sometimes avoid the bullies in the schoolyard. You could pretend you were eating chocolate cake when all there was in the house was potatoes and powdered milk. You could step around the needles on the lawn, the strung-outs and drunks hanging out all over the place. But what good was it to survive all of this when the Big One could happen at any moment? What was the point of surviving if people who didn't know any better had their fingers poised on little red buttons they could press on either side of the world, and it was as quick as the snap of a finger? Boom. Instant death. That's what got me at night. I'd lie around in bed thinking about all of the things I couldn't possibly stop, all the mistakes that people could make.

But worse than that, when the end came—and of course the bombs would be aimed at America, not us in Canada—the planet would become one gigantic bad neighbourhood overnight. PK and I had our escape route all planned out. How to hot-wire cars, which side roads to take to avoid traffic. We even figured out which highways could take us far enough north that we might be able to find some clean water. I stashed away some food in the boxes lining the floor. Just some canned stuff—beets, peanut butter, a tin of turkey. There was a knife on me at all times and one stashed under my pillow. There would be gangs, I figured, when the bombs fell, looking to get anyone and anything. PK and I practised kung fu moves that we saw on TV, so that when the time came we'd at least be sort of ready.

Meanwhile Jessie was obsessed. Totally freaked. I mean, she was ready to kiss her ass goodbye every time Reagan came up in conversation, let alone the real situation. So she started practising a plea to the world leaders. In the mirror, while washing the dishes, in the shower. She talked to herself all the bloody time. Sometimes she'd tell me and PK about it, and I mean she was pretty damned grandiose. I wanted to gag over some of it, but mostly she was pretty accurate. A letter to Yasser Arafat, and one to Castro. A letter to Ronald Reagan. A letter to the Soviet Union. Dear Mr. Reagan, dear Mr. Arafat. Dear Mr. Andropov: I'm too young to die. Dear men with little red buttons that we're not even sure will make a sound when they're pushed, at least not loud enough to warn us all the way over here, I have nightmares every night. I'm worried that I'm never going to grow up. You're so blind, so stupid. We hate you. We want you to die. We think you stink, you and your bombs. We've seen what they can do on TV. They have shows on what it would be like. Are you really that stupid? Is there any way we can stop you?

The spring before everything changed there was this day when the world was one gigantic soup bowl. The air had a funny feel to it, like it was charged up by batteries. That's what it felt like on our tongues. We were sitting on our portable steps at school, the three of us eating lunch together, and Jessie was spaced out, staring at the field that stretched behind the school.

So I started joking around, saying, "What's a'matter, Jess. You look like it's the end of the world or something." Apparently that was the wrong thing to say. She burst into tears. PK shot me death ray eyes and I suddenly felt like I should be crawling around eating dirt.

"Uh, Jeez, Jess, I'm sorry. Shit, I didn't mean nothin'—"

And she just sobbed, "I n-n-know. It's just, like, a bad dream I had," and rubbed snot on her raincoat sleeve.

PK, my bloody hero, put his arm around Jess. "It's okay, Jess. Everything's okay. You wanna tell us about it?" Jess just shook her head, sniffling and stuff.

"Really, Jess. You should tell us. It might make you feel better," I said. And so when she'd calmed down enough that her hiccups stopped she opened her mouth and it all fell out.

The worst thing, I guess, is that it started right there. Right on the very field that we were looking out at. At least it started out kind of good, if a little weird. In her dream Jessie was some sort of ghost. She was in this long flowing white nightgown, and she was flying over the field. There were all these kids from our class playing soccer in the mud puddles, kicking around a ball. So there's Jessie hovering over the game, only she's about to go over the field goal post when some of the kids start to notice her. And all the sudden they're waving their arms, shouting at her, only she can't understand them. It's a dream, right? So she wants to go down and ask them what's up, only she can't. Just as she's going over the field goal there's this really strong wind and it pushes her. It's like a magnet.

So Jessie has no choice. She flies over the goalpost. Only she's not on the school field any more once she's crossed it. She's flying over this city that's all shadowy and dark, like someone's turned out all the lights. There's a hot wind all around her, all dusty and filled with debris, and it scratches and claws her. Something's biting at her arms and stuff, and when she looks down at them it hits her: it *is* teeth. But they aren't attached to anything, they're just flying loose in the wind.

At this point in her story, I'll admit, I was feeling kind of sick. Where did she come up with this stuff? She tells us there's something pulling at her hand, and she grabs at it to look at it. But it isn't someone flying around out there like her. Oh no, that'd be way too simple. It's a bloody stump of an arm that's been burnt and torn off somebody. She's so freaked out—and it's a flying dream, so this makes sense—

that she can't fly anymore. She plummets to the ground, only it's not the ground anymore. The city has simmered down to glass and smoke and dust and huge burning craters. So Jessie tells us that she falls into one of these holes. But she knows she'll never get out. It's pressing her down, holding her in there. She's just going to burn alive, forever and ever.

So when it's over, when she's finished telling us her nightmare, the ever brilliant PK said, "Holy crap, that's bad."

"Jesus, Jessie."

"Yeah," she said. She looked like she wanted to start blubbering again so I put my arm around her, sort of rubbed her back a bit.

"It's okay, Jess," I told her. "It was just a bad dream."

"Like, I know it was just a dream—"

We were all kind of looking at the field like it was a person who'd suddenly taken all their clothes off. "Nightmares are supposed to be like that," PK said and pushed his glasses up on his nose. "They're supposed to stick with you. It wouldn't be called a nightmare if it didn't. It's the chemical traces in our brains." He put his arm around her other side, and we just sat there for a long time, ignoring our lunches and the other kids running around. As if we could eat after that one.

Jessie threw up her hands. I think she thought we weren't taking her seriously. "That's not the point," she said. "Just forget about it, okay?" But we did take her seriously. We just didn't want to admit it. I, for one, didn't want to talk about my own version of the apocalyptic nightmare.

But it was something else that kept me quiet. I mean, call me stupid but I hadn't put it together until just then. It finally dawned on me what was happening every night that Jessie climbed inside her closet and closed the doors behind her. She thought she'd be safe there. She thought that's how she could survive the end of the world.

I went over to Jessie's house for dinner that night. Her mom made this huge meal and we sat around telling her mom how much Michael Jackson sucked and how cool the Material Girl was. Jess was really starting to perk up again. As usual, her father had gone into the livingroom to watch the news, and me and Jessie were getting up to do the dishes.

I didn't know what it was—the hair stood up on her neck and she just sort of dropped everything. All I really saw was her ponytail sashaying out of the room. I said, "What's up, Jessie," but she didn't answer me. She was in her night time zombie routine. So I followed her into the livingroom.

We'd been watching a lot of news. Jessie's dad thought it was terrific. He'd nod at us, arms crossed over his chest, "Good for you girls. Keeping an eye on the pulse of things is very important." There'd been a lot of protests lately. People—i.e. me—were afraid that Canada was going to turn into the U.S.A's nuclear playground. A whole whack of people had marched from Canada to New York to try and prevent nuke testing in the north. But it didn't sound like Trudeau was going to let it happen. Trudeau wanted to get rid of all the bombs.

So anyway, this guy on TV was talking about President Reagan and the Soviet Union, and how some kid from the States had written the Russian President and asked him not to blow up the world. Jessie sat on the carpet like she'd gone into a trance.

They flashed this picture of a girl. She was just some little girl, all sweet and pretty. One of those kids you know are really well taken care of. Blue eyes like mine, brown hair like mine. Same age as us. Smith. Samantha Smith. I mean, I know there are like a bazillion Smiths in the world, but I still thought it was kind of funny, her having the same last name as mine. I remember thinking, maybe she's a relative.

Wouldn't that be something?

They flashed back to Reagan and some sort of speech he was giving on how Star Wars would make sure there was no nuclear war. Now Reagan—there was a guy who freaked me out but good. He reminded me of a Hallowe'en mask. His big orange juice grin, his beady, watery eyes. It was pretty obvious to me that he was the one who really was aching to lob the big ones.

"—the Soviet leader has replied to the letter, inviting the young Miss Smith to visit the Soviet Union this summer," the news guy said. His eyebrows lifted and crawled like he didn't believe a word he was saying. "This comes on the heels of Reagan's announcement of the Star Wars project, a global missile strategy aimed at defence against nuclear strikes from countries with burgeoning nuclear capabilities. The missile capacity of the Soviet Union..."

I sort of started mumbling to myself. I mean, why the hell didn't she write her own damned President? He was the guy in charge. He's the one who was getting everyone hot under the collar with his whole Star Wars deal. And then it hit me: "Hey Jessie," I said. "She stole your idea."

Her mom kinda gave me this look, like she didn't know what I was talking about. Jessie turned her head. Her hands were folded on her knees and I stood there in the doorway, a little spooked. Her face was all shiny with tears. And then she said, sort of smiling a bit, "I know."

Samantha Smith,
Manchester, Maine, USA

Dear Samantha,

I received your letter, which is like many others that have reached me recently from your country, and from other countries around the world.

It seems to me—I can tell by your letter—that you are a courageous and honest girl, resembling Becky, the friend of Tom Sawyer in the famous book of your compatriot Mark Twain. This book is well known and loved in our country by all boys and girls.

You write that you are anxious about whether there will be a nuclear war between our two countries. And you ask are we doing anything so that war will not break out.

Your question is the most important of those that every thinking man can pose. I will reply to you seriously and honestly.

Yes, Samantha, we in the Soviet Union are trying to do everything so that there will not be war on earth. This is what every Soviet man wants. This is what the great founder of our state, Vladimir Lenin, taught us.

Soviet people well know what a terrible thing war is. Forty-two years ago, Nazi Germany, which strived for supremacy over the whole world, attacked our country, burned and destroyed many thousands of our towns and villages, killed millions of Soviet men, women and children.

In that war, which ended with our victory, we were in alliance with the United States: together we fought for the liberation of many people from the Nazi invaders. I hope that you know about this from your history lessons in school. And today we want very much to live in peace, to *trade and cooperate with all our neighbors on this earth—with those far away and those near by. And certainly with such a great country as the United States of America.*

In America and in our country there are nuclear weapons—terrible weapons that can kill millions of people in an instant. But we do not want them to be ever used. That's precisely why the Soviet Union solemnly declared throughout the entire world that never—never—will it use nuclear weapons first against any country. In general we propose to discontinue further production of them and to proceed to the abolition of all the stockpiles on earth.

It seems to me that this is a sufficient answer to your second question: "Why do you want to wage war against the whole world or at least the United States?" We want nothing of the kind. No one in our country—neither workers, peasants, writers nor doctors, neither grown-ups nor children, nor members of the government—want either a big or "little" war.

We want peace. There is something that we are occupied with: growing wheat, building and inventing, writing books and flying into space. We want peace for ourselves and for all peoples of the planet. For our children and for you, Samantha.

I invite you, if your parents will let you, to come to our country, the best time being this summer. You will find out about our country, meet with your contemporaries, visit an international children's camp —"Artek"—on the sea. And see for yourself: in the Soviet Union everyone is for peace and friendship among peoples.

Thank you for your letter. I wish you all the best in your young life.

Y. Andropov

Killing the Messengers

We're feeling cozy, PK and me, at the cafe that serves us coffee and mashed potatoes for two-forty, with two slices of bread and a little packet of butter. I've got my feet stretched out on the patio, and we're sitting beside this huge tree growing right in the middle of it that seems a little unreal beside the busy street. And I'm just glad to be out of my head, out of bed, and back in the land of the living.

"So let me get this straight—Joe told you that nothing, absolutely nothing is going to be done to Jackson?" PK makes this face. It's almost like comic relief at this point, because I've been telling him the gory details of my flight from the Underground.

"Peek—I thought you were supposed to be the more cynical one. Of course they're not. Zach and me aren't even witnesses. No one asked us anything."

"Is the guy going to live?"

"He's not going to want to for a while. But yeah, I guess so."

"That's just so brutal. I mean—"

"Yeah, well. Listen. The whole thing just kinda makes me sick, so can we talk about something else for a while? It's not as if I want Jackson to go to jail or anything," I lie. Jackson takes good care of me in the club and on the streets. I know he'd beat some asshole to death if they touched me—even if it was a clubber. I've been feeling like a traitor, lying in my bed all sick and thinking, yeah, Jackson has it coming to him. He ought to go to jail. So how come I like knowing that he's looking out for me if I can't take him protecting the club? It doesn't make any sense, and I'm afraid to tell anybody what I'm really thinking. Even PK.

"Magpie. My dear." PK puts on his most disapproving face and looks at me mid-slurp of my coffee. I sputter, spit the now cool liquid back into the cracked porcelain cup. "You don't have to pretend with me. Remember me? Your best friend? Your better half? It's Peckoria here."

"Peek?"

"What," he says, examining the trees and what sky he can see overhead.

"Do you ever feel like a traitor?"

"Every time I wake up in the morning." I nod, keep nodding and nodding. I mean, I'll admit it—I have no clue what he's talking about. We aren't on the same page at all.

The pause is turning gray when I finally nudge him, "Go on already."

"I wake up and I think to myself, where the hell are you, PK? You know what I'm saying?"

"No."

He fiddles with his fork, lifting it back and forth across the potatoes, sifting through previous tracks, smoothing them down. Finally he plucks a humungous mushroom from the mushroom gravy.

"God, I'm so sick of this shit," he says. Personally, I'm trying not to watch him chew with his mouth open. "I mean, a story like that. Doesn't it make you a little tired of the scene?"

"Uh, yeah," I say, because right at this moment I catch Benny and Spanky out of the corner of my eye. Benny looks all faux-glamorous as he stops and flips up his shades to smile and say hi to people he knows, shoulders punched out of his dirty white undershirt and his long shorts riding awfully low. Spanky's shuffling past the tables like he knows his face is on the side of a milk carton.

"Hey, munchkins and lampoons. How's it hanging?" Benny flips up his shades like he's the poorest little rich guy in the world.

"About three inches lower than your waist, I'd say," and I'm flipping up my own shades and pretending I'm looking at his bare ass.

"Don't be lippy, Magpie," he smiles. I hate it when Benny smiles. It almost always means bad news. "Spanky, where are your manners?"

"Hi. Hi," Spanky says. He looks flustered and all the sudden I worry about what he's been up to with Mr. Bad Influence himself.

"Spanky, sit," PK says, ignoring Benny.

Benny puts this look on his face, this pouting martyr thing. "What—you don't want to see what I brung yous?"

"I'll bite," PK says, handing Spanky his cold cup of coffee, "what've you brunged us, Benny?"

Here Benny bends down between Peek and me, opening his legs wide and pulling something out of the hipster bag that he's seldom seen without. I don't like his shit-eating grin, so I say, "How much are you going to hand out for us, Benny?"

"Lean over like good girls and boys." And with a flourish of his hand, Benny produces a giant bag of mushrooms. This is all good, except that we're less than two feet away from the street and it would suck getting kicked out of the cheapest cafe in a four-mile radius of our hood. I look around, all paranoid, but if anyone sees they don't seem to care.

"Well?"

"Yeah, it's pretty, okay Benny? Now would you put it away? That looks like enough to mean trafficking." This is PK, with the same look in his eyes that says, what the fuck? What's this crazy shyster up to?

"Cheap deal today, friends. There's a party at me and mine's tonight. And I'll give you a score if you do some special invites—and give me ten bucks."

"How much of a score," I ask, and try to keep suspicion out of my voice.

"Weeeellll.... I already gave Spanky some freebs, four

grams. And as I have some business to attend to and I'll have to leave my good friend here to your devices, I suppose I'll hand you each four too. Sound like a plan?" So that, I think, is what's up with Spanky. He's totally high and it's like 11 in the morning. Mr. Bad Influence strikes again.

"Ahem," Peek says. "Deal for five bucks total." And I'm like, my hero. That's my man.

"Wait a minute—"

"Benny," I pipe in, "you haven't even told us who your special cruising mission's for. I dunno," and I'm all looking at my nails and shit, "maybe we had plans."

"Fuck off you had—Okay, look. Five bucks but you have to hightail it to Claremont and go to this address," and he hands us a slip of paper and an envelope, folded and marked with Benny's infamous martini stamp. "Ask for Vern at the door, tell him it's urgent, give him this. Got it?"

"I think we can handle it," I say in my best born-to-be-sarcastic voice. "But we need six g's each, Benny."

He pretends to think about it for a minute, pulls his sunglasses off and ponders the cafe like he knows he's getting ripped off and is trying to remain calm. But I know better—this means that we're probably getting fucked.

"Okay. Fine. You win, assholes. PK, follow me to the can in three minutes."

"What, you don't want to fix it up right here?" PK mouths off. And now I know that I've had too much coffee, because I start to see how we could just stir a few of those mushroom into the mushroom gravy. They'd probably taste better, and nobody'd know the difference, right?

"Forget it then."

"No, no. See you in a flash." Peek flashes some teeth at Benny, who drops from view, into the bowels of the cafe. PK smashes out the rest of his cigarette and beats a hasty path to the washrooms downstairs, saying, "Make sure you get our bill on the way out, eh?" And then I'm alone with the very quiet Spanky.

"You okay?" He looks splotchy, red and white, and if possible, even dirtier than before.

"Nahumph," he nods and shakes.

"What does that mean?"

"I'm okay," he finally mouths, sticking a hand over his mouth like he doesn't want to say it. "My mouse got hit by a car last night. Ran into traffic."

"Oh. Sorry."

"Got a new one this morning. Found her in the subway. She's a little bigger. Wanna see?" He pokes at his sleeve and a little black nose emerges, sniffing all the fabric in sight.

"Very cute. Whadda ya call this one?"

"Cleo. Like Cleopatra."

"Hell of a name to live up to for a mouse."

"Yah. Maybe." Spanky looks down and strokes the mouse's throat. I see a few uncomfortable glances from some Yuppies slumming it here at cheap-o cafe.

"Whew!" I raise my voice. "Good thing you caught that one before it got into the perogies!"

"What?"

"Nothin'. Just a joke." The Yuppies are packing up their cafe au laits and cakes and are half-way off the patio before I can smile cheekily in their direction. "So. Are you sure you can take care of this animal properly, young man?" It must have been the wrong thing to say because Spanky stuffs Cleo back into his sleeve and looks really embarrassed. Like he's not going to say another word to me ever again. "Spanky—I was just joking. I didn't mean anything by that."

He raises his head after a minute and I get a good look at his face. The red marks, the bruised crescents beneath his eyes. None too friendly eyes, at the moment.

"I always wanted a pet," he tells me.

"Yeah, me too."

"Did you ever get one?"

"Naw. Who would want to live in our crappy apartment?"

"I didn't ever get one either. We had room, though. We lived on the edge of town in this house. There was this huge yard."

"Oh yeah? Where was this?"

"Sudbury." I shiver exaggeratedly. I'm not sure where to go with this, but I can feel it, under the surface. There is definitely somewhere to go with this.

Finally I just ask. "So why couldn't you have pets?"

"Just wasn't allowed."

"Your family allergic or something?"

"Nah." He drops it And what he doesn't say is so much more clear, like a thinly disguised transsexual or a punk with braces. "I'll take good care of her, you know. Cleo won't get hit by a car like Martin did. I'll take real good care of her."

"I know you will. Hey. You want a coffee? Here. I know you do."

So we set out on our mission. Coordinates: Claremont and something or other. It really doesn't matter. It's obvious that we've made a silent agreement to take our sweet-ass time and make a day out of it.

We decide to stop in at some stores along the way and play our favourite game. It gives us a sense of satisfaction, lets us get back at all the wackos who think that every kid they see is evil and will steal everything that isn't bolted down. I mean, these are the same people who ignore us at counters in favour of any old harpy who walks in the door, the people who treat us like third-class citizens. Like we don't get enough of that everywhere else. These are the people who would be thrilled if the government decided to exterminate us outright. So they get a little mind-fucked. Oh well.

It goes like this: split up, see who gets targeted first, who gets asked to open their bag and show the nice security officer or undercover dick your lunch wrapped up in a brown paper bag or your roll of tampons. Points are given for stopping to examine small, easily liftable objects closely, then putting them back almost imperceptibly. The only other rule is that you must never, never ever, while playing the game, actually lift something. That would be like shitting in your own backyard.

We hit the big drugstore down on College, a hardware store where I swear the man actually hurts his neck trying to watch us all. And then—the *pièce de résistance*—the music store that's too low volume to have a proper security system.

"Can I help you? What is it that you're looking for today?" the man asks Peek. So Peek gets into this long, drawn-out conversation about the need to abolish the tape system and how he's really into this new age crap, and by the way, had he seen the new Dead Kennedys' album anywhere? Or Jello Biafra's solo stuff? What about Hawkwind's video collector's items... I mean Lemy, come on. This poor guy—he doesn't know what to think or who to pay attention to. He looks like he's going to blow his wad, what with Spanky looking like a cardboard box bum and me with my blue hair streaking all over the place. He gets visibly nervous when we drop out of view behind a rack. He fluffs up the hair around his balding temple, pulls on his belt, begins to hum and hah and forget sentences half spoken. This is his idea of inconspicuously suspecting us of swarm lifting. We, of course, fold our hands underneath the bins to make it look a little scarier. But here's the funny part—I'm watching some snot-nosed jock boy across the store stuffing his pants with CD's while this guy is busy watching us. Points for the kid.

I walk up to PK and say, "It's not here." And he says, "You're kidding. It's not?" "Nope." "Oh well, then," Peek sighs, "thank you for your time then, Sir," and we hightail it out of there. And then, just to make sure we don't get banned for life or wrongly accused or something, I turn back and go into the store. I motion to the dude, make him lean over while I whisper into his ear, "Hey man, I've been watching and well, I think you should pat that kid down, mister." I point kind of halfway to where the kid with the three hundred dollar jeans is perusing some serious rap. "He's a hell of a lot bulkier than when he walked in."

So we decide that we should probably make it to the Claremont address before sundown. It turns out to be halfway to the edge of buttfuck nowhere. Industrial warehouses with the glass blown out of the windows, run-down flops. It looks familiar, like our own hood only less people, and PK suddenly turns to me and says exactly what's on my mind.

"Hey, aren't you starting to get curious about what the hell we're carrying?"

"Don't even think about it," I tell him. "You fuck with that seal and he'll find out and kick our asses all over kingdom come."

"Yeah, yeah. I know. You're right."

"Can't you just replace the seal," Spanky says. He seems much calmer since the day's been wearing.

"Uh-uh." The thing with Benzadrine's seals is that everyone knows them, right? So if you break one, people can tell. The messenger's been burnt more than once, trying to peek to see if there were any drugs stashed to be bitten into. Everyone knows the code, see," I take the thing in hand and point out the various features of Benny's wax martini stamp that he had specially made for him. This one's red wax, which means no drugs included. Which means Peek and I are all the more interested in the contents.

The address turns out to be a large warehouse building with a 'FOR RENT/FOR SALE' banner slashed across the top. It looks deserted—wooden planks nailed across most of the windows. The door could be anyone's door, with its industrial handle and faded gold lettering reading *Dave's Good Motors,* so I'm thinking *crackhouse.* PK and I exchange a look while Spanky readjusts his new mouse.

"She okay?"

Spanky smiles, says, "Yeah. She's just settling into her new home."

"She's got to be boiling in there," PK says. "Shouldn't you get her a leash or something? Let her ride on your shoulder?"

"Mice like it hot. Anyways, they don't make leashes small enough for mice, do they?"

"You're right. I don't think they do."

We stand inside what I'm guessing passes for a small security lobby. And I'm looking around, thinking it would be great to have some warm armpit as a home, or something equally stupid. No cares in the world. The floor is heaped with a foot of grime and mud, the walls unplastering themselves. All the buzzers are ripped out of the wall panel except one. PK touches his finger to it and the tiny space echoes.

"What the FUCK do you want!" A not altogether pleasant beginning. Click. Our turn.

Peek goes, "Uh, we've brought a message for a guy named Vern? We were told to bring it to this address. Directly."

"Too bad." Click. We can hear them listening.

It's really hot and I can feel my bladder expanding with all that coffee. "Hey, hul-lo?" I yell at the ceiling. "Benny G. sent us? Told us it was urgent. We won't talk to anyone but Vern himself. Got it?" Click. The line goes dead. I hear us breathing in the stillborn air.

A few seconds later the voice comes back again. "Stay right there," it says, "I'm coming to get you."

I can't say for sure how Spank and Peek are doing, but I'm beginning to experience something akin to fear. It's not unusual to hear rumours about messengers who get caught in the crossfire of drug wars, turf wars. And Benny's known, but he's not all that big. I mean, he's not as operational as this dude seems to be. Whoever he is. And that's a point too. I've never even heard of this wacko. So we wait, a sweaty glob of bystanders, by the door.

A few minutes later a very large man appears. He's really buff, and I mean really. There's sweat pouring down his forehead, which makes me suspect that it's even hotter upstairs, or maybe it's a really long trip, to the top floor, maybe. The penthouse of the crackhouse.

So this gorilla guy steps out and slams it shut behind him. It makes a resounding thwang noise, like the springs are shot, and there's a whoosh of air behind him. Hair stirs up off my forehead.

"You have a message?" I recognize him as the one from the intercom.

"You Vern?" Peek says, trying not to look scared.

"What if I am?" Buff guy crosses his arms, pulls the bouncer façade. Familiar territory, I think to myself.

"Listen," I mouth off. "You ain't Vern, that's for sure. So why don't you tell us where he is." Sometimes I am so stupid.

He's got cold sores slathered all around his lips. He snaps gum loudly, blows a bubble. "No. I ain't Vern."

"We need to see Vern," I say.

"That depends on the message," Buff guy goes. But the

guy has a Palace Nightclub shirt on, so I can't really take him very seriously.

"Uhmm," I go like a stupid idiot. "I don't suppose you've got a bathroom up there, do you?"

"Why? You gotta fix real bad?" he says, but he's really disinterested. PK produces Benny's message and Buff guy peruses the marks. I start crossing my legs, wishing we didn't have to wait here so I could at least find an alley. Finally, after a frigging eternity of this guy flipping the note back and forth in the dirty light like he's going to discover it's fake ID he gives us this appraising look and says, "Okay. Let's go."

At this moment I think Spanky's the only one of us who doesn't seem completely fazed. Of course, he's got a look to him like the innocent lamb to the slaughter, and I start cursing Benny in my brain for getting us into this. I can't believe we actually gave him five bucks for this. I mean, what if this little piece of paper is actually a declaration of a drug war or something? Since we didn't peek we really can't be sure if Benny was on the level with us about anything.

Buff guy produces a wicked set of keys from the end of his chain that's tucked inside his tight black jeans that are all bulgy and shit—a key chain with a Hell's Angels insignia. Everything's beginning to look like the exact opposite of a harmless little party invite. And I'm thinking, Hell's Angels ain't no small-time shit. What's Benny up to now?

"Alright, listen mister," I say. "I ain't going up there until you can confirm to me that I ain't gonna have to piss myself when I reach the top of the stairs."

And he only grunts. "Let's go."

I take that as an affirmative. I mean, I'm freaked out, but at the moment I'm more concerned about peeing my pants. And so we walk up four flights of stairs that smell like baked vomit and shit.

It turns out that the floor we get off on is protected by yet another security guard, this time a blond guy who proceeds to pat us down and finds our shrooms. Luckily, in a crowd of dealers, these security people just smile and look them through, licking their fingers before letting us proceed. They think we're cute. The door we stop at looks like its been beaten down several times, all wrapped in wooden bandaids. Buff guy, his face shiny with exertion, knocks loudly on one of the bandaids and it opens into a dark room chilled in a half light.

It takes a few minutes to adjust to the gloom. The place is riddled with darkness and junk. There are holes in the plaster and one of those giant velvet paintings of cats playing pool on one wall. Red and green spotty blinds cover the far windows. Coke cans, pizza crusts, medical tubing litter the floor. A baby carriage trapped in one corner, decapitated Barbie dolls hanging from plumbing pipes at odd junctures. Shoved into one corner of the room is the furniture—a dusty and tattered orange velvet love seat and a ripped-up black leather couch. An easy chair, lazyboy style, mars another corner. A figure sits in it, bent low over the sixties style coffee table slathered in ashtrays overflowing with butts and the corpses of joints. Fixing gear and three needles sitting on the corner. And I'm thinking, Oh J.F. Christ, is he going to make us fix to get out the door?

"Yo," Buff guy announces. "These are Benny's kids."

"Yo," I say. "We ain't Benny's kids, alright? Does it look like we're adopted? We were in the hood and we're doing a favour, got it? Benny's kids got puncture wounds. See any on me?" I make a big production out of lifting the intact insides of my arms for inspection.

"Whatever," Buff guy counters. "Shut up."

"Well, that can change," lazyboy guy starts to get up.

"What's the message."

Peek walks a few steps up to the guy and stops when Buff guy looks like he's going to pull a piece. "It's right here," he says, stopping dead. "Benny told us to deliver it to Vern."

"That would be me," the guy says. Vern standing up is ludicrously tall and skinny, absurd looking. He's got the long face and chiselled cheeks of an underfed giant, the large sockety eyes of a fish. He saunters over to us in his dirty pants and smelly shirt with this hunched rockstar attitude.

"Yeah. So. Whatever. It's just a party invite—that's what Benny said, anyhow. Can I use your bathroom?" Vern's eyes go hooded with delight, and he looks over my arms again, flicks them over my face and down towards my crossed legs. There's a smile hovering somewhere near the vicinity of his mouth and I don't even really catch it when he nods at Buff guy, who tells me to follow him. We walk down a black hallway that I hadn't noticed before. No windows, closed doors on either side that let in no light. Down at the end of the hall is a door with just the tiniest glint of light coming from underneath. Buff Guy grabs my shoulder and points to the door, saying, "No funny stuff," just like out of the worst fucking movie, "and hurry up."

I'm thinking, faster than you even know how to spell it, friend, and tiptoe my way past him to the door where a ripe smell of men and shit wafts through. I turn the rickety knob and have to push as hard as I can at the warped wood. This is one of the worst experiences of my life, I think, as I try to cop a squat over an overflowing and stuffed-up toilet bowl stained a dark brown by who the fuck knows what. I actually have to cover my face to stifle the gag reflex that threatens to make me retch before I can get my pants down. That's when it hits me to be really afraid for us. These guys are fucking looney tunes. They've got to be totally cracked. My skin prickles all over, a sudden chill accompanied by the knowledge that Benny will so PAY for this. My guts twist with panic, wondering if we'll get out with our skins still on. At least I now know why Vern was smiling when I asked to go to the bathroom. And now I know why Benny gave in so easy on the drug price. We are such suckers. Fucking prick.

When I return to the fray, looking, I'm sure, white and clammy like someone with DT's, Spanky and PK are standing ready beside the door. "Uh—thanks for the use of your—uh— facilities." The note is there beside Vern, open. I can almost make out Benny's chicken scrawls. But Vern's uninterested. He's busy fixing.

"Hey, no problem," he lifts an arm and drawls. "Take it easy." We all try to walk casually out the door only to drop, once we reach the stairs, into a dead run. It's like coming out of a basement, feeling something pulling at your hair and clothes.

So Spanky goes, "How much is four grams in the other kind of measurement? Would it be four litres if it was liquid? Or how many pounds?" We pop our shrooms just before twilight and find ourselves in another warehouse part of town. I can't drag my eyes away from all the broken windows, graffiti, patches of weeds and peeling plaster. We wander, wide-eyed, sleepy and vibrantly awake, carefully skimming our way past buildings with people inside, trucks and cars parked out front. This is the time I like best, I suppose, because nothing's finished yet. Under the orange glow of dusk the buildings cool off like the heater on a cigarette. It's like the last kick before you turn white and your eyes roll back into your head.

I can't comprehend at all, so I go, "You're uhm—overana-lyzing, Spanky."

Peek cocks his head as though he's trying real hard to listen. "You know," he finally says, "I don't know that? That's funny. Don't you think that's funny, Magpie?"

"Uhm. Yeah." There are huge gaps between our words, a stuttering of the brain. My limbs are starting to pulse and feel all light then heavy, as though concrete is circulating through them instead of blood.

Spanky stops at a post that's missing its sign and twirls around on it. "Hey Magpie, where'd you get you name 'Magpie'?"

"Hey Spanky. Where'd you get your name 'Spanky'?"

"Kids on TV," Peek chimes in.

I point to myself and smile. "Kids on crack," I say. This cracks Spanky up. It's great to see him all doubled up with laughter, looking like a kid. Peek is smiling too. I can practically see empathy rolling off his body like perspiration.

A street turns into a long, empty one-wayer. The sun is hitting just the tips of the buildings now, everything beneath losing its colours. There's a sprawling abandoned warehouse at the end of the street, most of the glass blown out of the windows. "If that building was a person," kind of surprised to hear my own voice, "it would be a bum." So obviously we're going in.

Inside it's the kind of massive space that makes me sad. I mean, here's all this room. But it's just sagging, broken-down room. It's off limits. It's untouchable, even though it's here, just waiting for someone to fill it up and throw it parties. I hear Spanky from behind me, "I could live here."

"Me too," Peek adds.

"Me three."

Spanky comes out of nowhere and stands in front of me. "Why don't we?"

"'Cause it would suck to move shit in here and then get

kicked out by bums or cops or pushers," I say.

"Magpie's right," PK says behind him. "We'd have to hide all the time, wouldn't be able to turn on any lights. Fucking freezing in winter." And then he thinks about it for a second, says, "I'm quite sure this space must already be spoken for."

"It's worth a try, isn't it?" Spanky says. "This floor can't be any more uncomfortable than the park. Probably better in winter."

"Spanky," I sigh. There is an overwhelmingness to it all. Spanky—see, Spanky isn't one of those loudmouth street kids, the kind who basically grew up on the streets and talk the talk. He probably came from a 'good' family, a place where there's grass and trees and maybe even a lake or two. But he was probably always standing just a little outside it all. The kind of kid who was always being forgotten when it came to pictures, or the one who's always standing right at the edge of the frame. He doesn't get the street yet. Maybe he never will. And while he doesn't, he's like a baby bird, vulnerable and sweet and not tough enough. And I don't have the words, or the heart, to explain it to him. It's like trying to tell a bad junkie that he's going to die.

We end up exploring the whole damned place. Where I'm standing the windows have been torn mostly open, exposing a slice of deepening blue and white. The moon's up already, even though it's still kind of light out, looking like an earring someone dropped in a pool.

"It's fucking depressing," I call out. I watch them tripping out by themselves. Every few seconds the flint of PK's glasses disappear, reappear, surfacing like lantern light off an old-fashioned train. Spanky's hands are leaving trails. He's flapping around in the dark and I'm thinking about his cheeks when he laughs. Sweet, round bubbles. I've seen his type before. I know what happens in this scenario. And I feel pretty damned helpless to do anything about it.

"Can you imagine," Peek says, "this place as a roller rink? Or a shelter?"

"No," I snort. I mean, what's the use of imagining things that are never going to happen? Usually I'm the optimistic one. But the whole day has just been creepy and sad. And I'm thinking of Spanky, and for some reason he reminds me of Jessie. And I can't seem to find the words to say it, even, which doesn't make me feel any better.

The last of the day's light is leaking through the windows and this bums me out too. I'm feeling like a weed growing out from between cracks in pavement. I feel like a pothole, like an accident. It's a bad trip.

"Peek."

"Yeah, Magpie."

"I think I'm hungry," I say.

"Yeah, me too." Spanky sits down on the dirty concrete like one of the lost boys and I go, "Man these shrooms are bad. I'm so bummed." And I shake my head, shiver all over, because I so don't want to go there.

We arrive at Benny's pad with pasty mouths and tracers of red and yellow buzzing off our hands. It's not late but the party has the look of a wild mosh pit already. Festoons of silver paper garnish the large room that opens into an industrial-type kitchen at the far end. It's the kind of place that could be classy if he ever got rid of the bunny babe pictures with their pouting and dripping red mouths topped with teased blonde hair (with black roots) and ridiculously large breasts.

Benny lives in a loft at the edge of our mad world, the kind of place that only a drug dealer could afford. And he throws the kind of parties that only a drug dealer could afford. Music I hardly recognize is playing on the DJ's turntables. A dude is spinning and scratching some kind of techno ambient groove designed for the psychedelically impaired.

But for all the wealth of Benny's loft, there's a lack of furnishings. The kitchen looks empty, sterile. The livingroom's bare with only a long, L-shaped corduroy couch and a few chairs. The rest of the loft is dotted with empty beer kegs fashioned with wooden seat tops. Bongo and tam drummers have arranged them into a neat circle and drum to the beat—just the kind of wanker crap I hate. These dudes are so obviously Benny's weed clientele. At this point Benny spots us and hightails it over.

"So friends, how was the mission?" He's obviously wasted, poured inside some tight black metal tee and silver pants, silver sprayed platform boots, holding one of his insignia martinis in one hand and a breast in the other.

PK raises a hand to his forehead and salutes. Spanky watches and attempts a lamer version. "Mission complete, Captain," Spanky tells him.

"Well," I say like a wise-cracking asshole, "I had a bad trip."

"Did he say anything to you? Is he coming tonight?"

PK puts on this fake apology face. "Sorry, man. He didn't even read it in front of us."

"Oh yeah, right. But didn't you tell him about the party? I told you to invite him."

I'm losing my cool now. "You told us to deliver the message, Benny. I didn't hear jack shit about singing telegrams."

"Whatever," Benny snorts and his lips curl in disgust.

And I can't help it. I'm so pissed off that I just blurt it out. "You look like a fucking pimp, Benny," I tell him. And it's true. The breast he's holding belongs to a leggy, spaced-out brunette. Her lipstick's smeared all over her lips like she's been involved in a tonsil swapping session with the corduroy couch. Benny's got his hand draped over her shoulder and over her basically exposed tit and she's acting like she's been freebasing way too much coke or some shit. So when I say this he actually squeezes her flesh a little tighter. I want to fucking ralph.

"Fuck you too. Bitch."

"Not only that, Benny, but you fucking owe us bigtime for that trip. Okay? So don't give me that mouthy garbage. What do you think Joe and Pete would say if they knew about our little 'mission' today, huh?" But really I'm thinking about Jackson. I'm kind of wondering: if it came to me and Benny, who's side would he take? Who would he protect? The drug dealer or the mouthy kid?

He smiles, and it's a little too comfortable for my liking. I look behind him, hoping to see my brothers. Benny's not all that good to be around when he's freaking and paranoid. But I guess we get off kind of lucky because he just says, "Enjoy the party," and turns around with this ho glued to his silver side and walks over to some other people.

When he's safely out of earshot PK leans over to me and whispers, "Someone should tell Benny about his fashion victim status." And I'm trying not to giggle, but hey, mushrooms are funny, and then we're both openly laughing until I catch Benny turning around to glare at us like he's capable of reading our thoughts. A sobering thought. So we take Spanky and sway into the fray, expecting the best, hoping for the worst.

Where are you, Peek? Right here. *What's that?* Beside you, right here. See? Feel my hand? *Yeah. Where are we, Peek?* I dunno. Somewhere in the Mediterranean, I'm guessing. *How do you know?* It's hot. Morocco hot. *Long distance runners, huh?* Yup. That's the shit.

Time is standing still inside this room, or so I think until I see a watch on someone's faceless wrist that lights up and tells me that it's a little after two. We're all awake, or so I think, but I'm not sure. I'm on the couch maybe, PK apparently still beside me, and we're sweating like pigs. Benny leans over me. *I'm on the couch, Benny*, I say. Yeah Magpie, I can see that. *Magpies don't really have blue feathers. Isn't that funny, Benny? I don't even think bluebirds have blue feathers. Nothing has blue feathers. Are you mad at me, Benny?*

My teeth are chattering like I'm freezing to death. My back and armpits are soaked with sweat. My forehead is sticky with it. Nawww, he says. The guy showed. I'm here to give you a treat for being such a good girl. Open up.

I tilt my head back and the room does quick, jarring pirouettes. I stick my tongue out and something sticks to it. *Whaw isth ith, a mawrble?*

Nawwwww, Benny says.

Toungk clampb?

Naaaawwwww. Ssswwwaaalllooowww.

A piece of paper. It sticks to the tongue and the back of the throat. It just sits there, the fibers turning soft and gushy in my throat, expanding and coating the part that's all narrow, maybe even the vocal chords. I try to say something but nothing comes out. This huge shadow glides over the walls that are like ancient faded movie screens. And even though that small part of my mind that's still intact sees that it's the drug dealer, Vern, I'm fucking freaking. He looks like a fucking cadaverous giant.

Peek. PK, wake me up. I'm having a nightmare.

What?

A bad *nightmare, Peek. Pinch me, dammit.* I feel this pressure on my arm, but it's like I imagine flesh that doesn't belong to you any more feels. My limbs aren't responding to stimuli. *Harder, Peek. Fuck.* It doesn't help. The shadow looms over me, folding over where the ceiling meets up with the wall.

Fuck, Peek we've gotta get outta here.

For some reason it sparks me off into the nightmare that's been playing over and over in my head since the night Jackson laid into that dude at the Club. The same damned nightmare as before. And I'm fucking wigging. I'm a wreck.

You're tripping, Mags.

No I'm not.

Yeah, you are. Benny slipped us some acid.

I feel his hand grabbing me, and suddenly they're both hot and sweaty. *Oh. I thought it was a tongue strangler. I thought he was trying to get me to shut up. He fuckin' betrayed us, man.*

PK just laughs a bit. It sounds a bit like a cawing bird. Acid, Mags, he says. You're just trippin'. It's all in your head.

What's this? I say, suddenly confused by the sweaty heat ball emanating off the ends of my limbs.

It's my hand. Jesus, Mags. Don't have a bad trip or anything.

Don't trust that Benny, Peek. Benny equals bad news. Somethin's up with him, eh?

PK looks around, over his shoulder. Hey, he says, will you have a care for our continued safety and please shut up?

PK, we need a change of scenery, I say. The shivers go up and down my back, the kind that feel like barbeque sauce is being sapped out of the spine. My heart is starting to beat like a bird's—fast and freaky. I lead him and me to the ladder stairs. Benny's got a bedroom built on stilts, and it's red and warm and has a window that looks down on all the action. It's like a playhouse. We're sliding up the ladder and I can't wait to look out the window. Suddenly I'm freaking tired. The all over tired shiver that I know is just the drugs jumping out of my system. *Today was such bad news. I'm so having a bad trip*, I tell PK, who grins his shit-eating grin at me.

He tells me, You've got a flair for overstatement.

Shut up, Peek, I say, and lead him over to the bed.

I don't know why but it all just comes flying out of my mouth. It feels like the bed is swallowing me, licking my flesh. *So—like—I'm feeling better up here*, I start, rubbing my hands up and down and grabbing at the red bedspread that feels sweet under my skin, but I know it belongs to sleazy Benny so I'm trying not to enjoy myself too much. What the fu-fuck are you talking about? Peek is starting to shiver now, too. I mean, I don't know if they're really good drugs or really bad ones.

I mean. There's nothing. Gonna freak me out. Up here, I say. I flick my hand against Peek's chest and he knows I want a cigarette. He pulls one out, sticks it between my teeth and lights it. A ball of blue flame that comes off the end of it until I puff. I'm suddenly feeling strong enough to let go of the com-forter, at least one of my handfuls, and smoke properly. *Member all those bad dreams*, I say, *member Peek, member?* And he says, Magpie, you've been telling me your dreams since you were as tall as my asshole. And I'll have you know, I think you're a sick fucking puppy. *Shut-up-prick.* I hit him on the chest and he stops laughing at me, at least for a second.

Member Jessie?

Yeah, of course I rem-member Je-ssie.

My brain rolls over itself and I'm all flashback style, and it's horrible, staring at Benny's red walls. Benny the traitor. Benny who's gonna get us all fucked up one of these days. And I'm thinking about this nightmare. I mean, it's so old. But it keeps coming back to stick me in the ass and I can never quite wrap my head around it.

Mags, I think you're getting a little distracted, I hear PK, and he's pulling on my earlobe and stealing my fucking cigarette.

And I go, *listen, you cheap bastard—*

All right all right, he says, and from the corner of my eye I can see him crossing his arms over his chest and he's trying to listen, he's trying.

So I spill. I tell him about finding myself in Jessie's room again. It's dark out, night-time, I guess. There's moonlight dribbling in even though I can't see the moon. And I'm just standing there, alone, and I hear her whisper, "Magpie? 'S'at you?"

"Yeah, Jessie, it's me."

"C'mere," she says. Her voice is coming from the closet. She's inside the closet again. I expect to find her sleeping. I press my face against the slots to see. Her hands are right there, and her eyes, peering back at me. Like she's in a cage. And she goes, "Soon, Magpie, soon. It's happening. You should come in here." And it's like I don't understand but I do. I'm scared. Fucking terrified. "Quickly, hurry up!" Her voice is getting all urgent.

So what's the point, Sherlock? Peek is propping the lids of his eyes open now, trying to stay focused. You sh-shouldn't have tea before bed any more?

And then, I say. There's this siren. One of those sirens that were installed in the fifties or something. The emergency broadcast sirens. I go over to the window and look out. I don't see anything, nothing but a bright, lopsided moon hanging out over the houses. It looks like it's upside down. I turn back—I'm about to ask Jessie what the deal is, when I spot someone sitting on her bed. A girl, about Jessie's age. She's all calm, just sitting there, her hands clasped in her lap. She turns her head to me, just her head. Says, "It's no use."

"What do you mean no use," I ask. Her eyes are all bright in the light, they're shiny and wet looking.

"It's no use. It's too late. It's over," she says. Her head turns back. She's looking at the closet door, and now Jessie's banging on it, banging like the hounds of hell are after her. Jessie's starting to scream and scream, and between that and the sirens I can't hear a damned thing.

I try to turn back to the window, waiting for all the noise to stop when I suddenly see it. It blooms out over the tops of the buildings, far away, like a flower growing in fast forward. The upside-down moon goes red, like someone's spilled red wine all over it, and the flowering light overtakes it, and it's gone. The moon's just swallowed. And there's only the white, white light. And it's blinding. For a moment I look back at the girl on the bed. She's staring at it all, not even wincing. I think I see tears tracking down her face, and she's whispering something, I can hear it over the din, "Too late now."

It's when I'm watching her that it happens. And I'm telling PK about how the room shatters with all this light. I mean it's all falling apart. We're being knocked into atoms quicker than I can blink, and it's so hot, I can feel the flesh slipping off my skin like it was a pair of rubber gloves. The light—it just gobbles us whole. And then there's nothing.

Peek grabs his forehead like his brains are spilling out. Whoa Mags, you're getting all trippy on me. I have no idea if he's being sarcastic or not at this point, but I'm in such a rush to get it all out I don't cross-examine.

Yeah. Well, that's what this dream is like, man. It's the fucking apocalypse.

Hang on, I gotta get us an ashtray. He comes back carrying a beer bottle. The butt splashes and fizzles out loudly. He goes, so let me get this straight. You think there's some sort of significance to this all?

Bigtime.

It's coincidence, Mags. Jess was on your mind. That's all.

But you know who it was? The other girl?

Madonna? He points at me like he's in some guessing game. Dorothy Parker.

That girl, Peek. Remember the girl?

What girl? He's looking at me like I've lost my mind and he's wondering if we should check me into the hospital.

So I add—*Her. The letter girl. Samantha Smith. It was her,* I say. And I'm really fucking tripping now because it's like she's always there, in the dark, waiting for me to turn to her and realize that it's all over.

His eyes sort of narrow, and he's all quiet for a minute. I can actually see the chains creaking in there, and I know the minute he gets it. And I'm freaking relieved. He fucking gets it.

Fu-uuuck, Mags. Really? He pushes his glasses up on his nose a bit, looking at me real serious and intent now.

Yeah, Peek. And you know how that turned out.

F-f-fuuuck.

The end of the fucking world, I say, and watch the red walls drip like candle wax down past the ladder, down onto the floor, into the dirty raging party.

Eat Yer Young

PK goes, "I'll tell you why." The tiny restaurant buzzes with grease and an electric twinge. We're drunk and alone after our debauch this evening. The red vinyl booth is quiet and the potatoes are cold hard lumps of poison, the coffee lukewarm. It's four a.m., maybe only three-thirty. Time lost meaning hours ago, when we were finally thrown out of the Underground. I pick at a hole in the ketchup pooled on my plate to view the cracks where pepper grains hide. The waitress looks bored, as usual, twirls her hair around a finger every few minutes with a concentrated attention I almost admire. Her fingers are stained like imperfect grapes. She looks about fifty but I happen to know she's only thirty-four. Nancy. Waitress Nancy. Her name tag reads 'Marie'.

"I'll tell you why." I've forgotten the question. Spanky and Derek and Benny have left, Nat went home ages ago. Zach and Pete and Joe were gone even before that, headed to a drinking can.

'Nancy' wears thick glasses, even thicker than PK's. Everything about her is thick. Her sweater, the sweats across her thick, pillowy thighs. Her thick, duck-like waddling. Her thick, stained fingers. She's thick.

The restaurant is run by her father, which is why I know that Nancy is not Marie and she's younger than she looks. Her father has cheekbones that look like they've been carved out of granite, and an Eastern European accent to match. Open since 'forty-nine, he's proud of telling me. Open all night, 365. This place is back in fashion. But not Nancy, I think unkindly. She was never in fashion. Even her father came back into vogue—her stern father who never cracks a smile except every now and then at the old boys ringing round the counter. Her father who bends over the steaming, smelly grill and places his hand flat down on the steaming metal. I saw him do this once. Really. I figured he just wanted to feel something. Something real and tangible after six hundred years of thankless struggle to get back into vogue with the young folks. Six hundred million nights of being unable to enjoy sunsets as he sets the grills, flips his burgers and puts dark brown edges onto now cold home-fried potatoes. Her father somehow made a comeback and is now a hipster's icon, the man we watch as he tests the grill. The man singeing his fingertips brown and nerveless, a lit cigarette perched in his mouth. Not Nancy, who went about waitressing as though she was sucking back an empty can of whipped cream and waiting to explode. An opaque backdrop floats in the air above her, layers of grease and smoke. The smell of a city almost lulled to sleep outside the painted front window and original leather seats from 'forty-nine.

I don't really mind that the potatoes have gone cold and PK goes, "I'll tell you why."

"Why what, already?"

"Why people bother. The whole job-kids-marriage-divorce and death thing." His eyebrows look arch.

"I'm *dying* to know."

"It's simple."

My eyes are heavy with drinking, the weight of being too young to hold it all in. Sparkly and dead tired. I have a blister on my heel the size and shape of Manhattan. "Shoot."

"Why do people pretend they're in love? Why do they get married, place this incredible faith in each another? Stick with shitty family lives, work their even shittier jobs and stay in places like this, pretending that everything's okay?" PK leans over, getting all into the conversation. "I get it. I really do. I was sitting there thinking about it in the club."

"Get what?"

"That they're all so fucking scared. They want to have all the normal things, so maybe they won't have to grow old and die alone. Retirement and kids ringing around their death bed is supposed to be their eternal reward. They don't want to know that their lives are going to be sucked up by all this useless shit. They're wrong, though. See? Don't you get it? It's not exactly the most original idea in the world, I'll admit," he blinks, frowns. I can see the wheels in his head churning at about the same speed as my stomach. "Only some of us hope we've found a new way to come at the problem. That death is inevitable. We all gotta die alone, regardless."

"Peek, man. You're getting a little too philosophical even for me right now."

"No—think about it. Love, lovers, war, commercials that tell you to reach out and touch someone before it's too late? It's all about covering up the facts, of trying to plaster it over. It's about creating a false victory over death, to hide the real truth of their existence. The happily-ever-after syndrome, only you and I both know that there's no such thing as a happy ending."

"Got any proof? What about... Grizzly Adams?"

"Come on, Mags. I'll start quoting Thoreau if you're not careful." And then he's back into his tirade: "This isn't exactly new. It's a mistake to think this is at all original. It's how people are going about it now that's changed."

We've been talking around this subject for like a year. Peek and I have been trying to figure out why some people think they can lead these supposedly normal lives. Get jobs, make some babies, grow old. It's hard for us to imagine how they can fool themselves into thinking that everything isn't complete shit, and everything else isn't a lie. And how would we really know, anyways, if this is any different than before? No one recorded the thought of a fourteen-year-old factory worker who died of rotted lungs, or the eighteen-year-old who got crushed in an 'accidental' mine explosion. Or picture a woman about my age whose boss rapes her—she gets pregnant and fired, and she and her kid die in the streets, completely anonymous. It must have happened more often than not, just like here, just like now. But it's hard to feel pity except for ourselves. And anyway, we never thought we'd make it this far. I mean, as far as we figured, we'd all be dead in like 1984.

The one time we'd thought: okay, things are looking up, things are getting better—it all blew up in our faces. That was around the time that Samantha Smith was hightailing it around Moscow, visiting some big kids' camp and singing songs with Russian kids. Jessie and Peek and me sat around watching reporters ask her, "So, like, is the Soviet Union going to lob the nukes?"—as if she could answer that. And all the while Samantha was globetrotting it, the gang in Washington were calling Trudeau a 'commie pinko' for trying to do the same thing.

But this kid got away with it. People couldn't get enough of her. We saw her on Letterman. She was interviewed by Tom Brokaw and Diane Sawyer. They threw her a frigging parade. I mean, everyone wanted to throw Samantha Smith a party, including the Soviets.

We lived through 1984, so I guess it worked. The guns were blazing but the bombs didn't fall, even though India started making bombs from the Candu reactor that was supposed to help the poor. Grenada was invaded, Britain went to war with the Falklands. The U.S.A. and the U.S.S.R. duked it out but somehow there was this buffer—this American kid with shining eyes and a huge, dimply smile standing between them, making the countries act like gentlemen as if she was the political version of Shirley Temple.

"Think about what's on the street right now, Mags. The acid's laced with PCP. The fucking pure H that's floating. Do you honestly believe that if the government really wanted us to stay off this shit there'd be any around? Reagan only started that whole 'just say no' shit because he wanted to own several small countries. Drugs that deliver us back into the wide hands of all-unknowing. We know too much, we have too much time to think. And we don't like to sleep alone because we know what's coming. So they promote it—lull the poor and then the rests of the folks into a false sense of living. Or they start gang wars to kill us all off, keep us where they want us. It's so obvious."

"Divorce is on the rise, PK. Marriage rates are low. Explain how that fits in."

"Sure it fits."

"How?"

"Why get married, procreate, when you know there's no point anymore?"

"What the hell are you talking about, Pekoria? I thought you just said—" I may be drunk, but even I know that his argument is starting to get a little fucked up.

"I'm talking about the existential dilemma. The poor had it figured it out years ago. We're alone, we're going to die alone and miserable, and we're not going to like it." He's slamming his finger on the table, punctuating each point in a way that makes my head throb. "We know what's coming. There's nothing left but to smoke the crackpipe at this point. Our culture is at the point of extinction."

"For Christ's sake, Peek, speak English."

"People gotta try before they give up. They gotta reach for the brass ring to justify their behaviour—the fucking sports cars, the cottage on the lake. People need their little fantasies." He shakes his head and leans back into the cracked leather. It's like he's gotten on a carousel and I'm just watching him go around and around.

"We can't get out of our heads," he says. "We can't pretend any more that there's any hope. You, Magpie. You think *this*," he starts pointing around at the clientele of the cafe, mostly old drunks looking for a wee bite before they continue their bingeing, "is sympathy—." He's actually and seriously snipping at me.

"Shut the fuck up, Peek, before you say something you'll regret."

"—The club, the dancing. You think it helps you wake up in the morning because there are other people like you. What a fucking sham."

"I believe in the collective unconscious," I say.

"That's bullshit. It ain't true."

"What is true then, Peek? Why don't you tell me, you fucking hypocrite."

"The bragging, the drinking, the drugs, the dancing, the sex. The growing up too fast and too fucking hard. And what is that?" He's flailing his arm around now. I know I'm in for it. "This isn't original. We haven't created a sympathetic society, Mags. We're just stuck in a hopeless caste system that endlessly repeats its mistakes until everything collapses under the weight of its own rotten foundation. And then everyone has the gall to think that this has never happened before. That 'we're so evolved'."

"Oh! Well, then. Fine. Why don't we all just kill each other."

"What do you think this is, Mags. The art of living well? Just look around you. Look at Nancy."

The sight of globby, gelatinous potatoes surrounded by pools of droopy ketchup are starting to make me feel seriously sick.

"*Light*-en *up* a little."

"Oh, that's right. Don't complain. Stick to what you know. Maybe, you know." His blinking slows down and stops. He stares out the window, fixated on something. Maybe at the lightening mauve of the sky. "That would be a nice thing to know, that I'm full of shit and all this," he spreads his hands out to include the table, the restaurant, the bums drinking their coffee in the corners, "this is just a fantasy of mine."

"You love the club."

Peek sighs. "Of course I love the club. It's exhilarating to think of all those people decked out and waiting for the end of the world."

But it isn't just the club. We both know it's more than that. We know, PK and I, why he can make it to University and I can't. We know why we won't bother to get married if we live long enough. It's not just about what the rest of the world is doing. It's not about people starving in China. It's about us, in the here and now. Nobody's ever going to give us a fighting chance at anything. To be honest, I just don't want the world to chew us to bits before it's done with us—at least, no more than it already has. And then I think about that kid in front of the club. What if PK's right, and all of this—the club, for instance—exists only to help them eat us alive?

"Everything turns to shit just as we get our hands near it," I say, and smack the potatoes with the fork that still bears the marks of last night's gravy.

"There's no difference between them and us," Peek says like he's just become the King of the Smartasses. Nancy cracks her gum with a loud snap next to the fifties cash register. Her eyes have the vacant look of a cow. She swaddles a strand of her stringy brown hair around her finger. I really hate her at this moment. I hate her so much I could kill her myself. And then Peek says, "The only difference is that we know exactly how disinherited we are. We *know* we're in the belly of the machine."

Seatbelt Sign

There have been a million days like this: days where your ass sticks to your seat, your thighs gummy, your head baking. Where you just have to sit back and drink the day away because there's nothing else to do and you're too hot to try even if there was something. Nat and I sit on this rooftop patio with its awnings and an actually cool wind. She knows people who work here, which is why I can get served, and every half hour or so the server guy who likes her comes over to chat her up.

She plays a cool game, Nathalie. Server guy's checking her out and grins as though he's got something on us before she smiles that 'not now I'm busy' look to let him know it's time to go. And he does. This is the amazing thing. It's as if she puts her thoughts right in the air between us, where the guy can sniff them. They always do what she wants, when she wants. Truly amazing.

Nathalie is one of the few 'cool' women that I can stand. Sure, she works as a barwench at one of the most annoyingly cool clubs. She has the requisite dyed black hair, the leather minis, the porcelain complexion and not last nor least an amazing bod. But she's also got a flakey but good heart when she's not playing tramp 'n' vamp. Seeing as how she's twenty-four it's nice of her to go out of her way to make time for me.

So we find ourselves alone, on the rooftop patio where I haven't been ID'd, where for once Nathalie is making an effort to impart something useful to me about life, the universe and everything. A delicate operation, as usual. She makes as many references to astrology as she does to her pet weasel, Eli. "So listen, Magpie Honey. You've got that drive, right? And that whole Aquarian thing with thinking too much about stuff that you can't do anything about. But then you've also got that carefree attitude. You gotta check that, y'know?"

This is where she adjusts the silver choke collar around her neck, rubs her hands up and down her arms where her tattooed raven perches beside a very colourful Minnie Mouse. I can see out of the corner of my eye men at the surrounding tables almost lick their lips when she moves. Nathalie has the kind of face that actually eclipses her body. The kind of rich blue eyes that get men and women gushing about china dolls. Innocent eyes under all that hair. But then her lips. Full-bodied, round. I might mention that I've never been jealous of Nat because she's got a terrible track record with men. She always goes out with losers. Like the last one— a guy named Spike or something who nicknamed *himself*— which is about the most uncool thing you can do—after his favourite occupation. Junk.

"Then Eli—I swear to God—" she's telling me, putting her bejewelled hand over the plastic heart patch on her shirt, "—jumped off the counter and right onto this dude's head! Started scratching him to bits. It was way cool and so I go—"

"Hey, Nat?"

"What."

"Why do you go out with all those losers?"

"Hey girlfriend. Chill on the attitude."

"Well I don't mean that exactly. But I mean you always check their signs ahead of time and there's still not a decent guy in the whole damned bunch."

"Yeah." She scrunches up her cute little nose and I swear I can see grown men swooning all around us. "Weird, isn't it." She tilts her head about, like she's pondering this deep life mystery.

"What about Derek?"

"What about him." She automatically gets this annoyed look, smooths a hand across her perfectly coiffed hair.

"I think he likes you."

"I think he likes wanking off to pictures of his mother. So?"

"So I think you like him too. Don't you?" I have a picture in my mind of the two of them at the club. Nat shows her true colours when she's drunk. I see them flirting all the time. Frankly, I think they've been sleeping together on the sly. And honestly, I'm asking more out of curiosity than anything else.

"Whatever. He's a fucking tool, Magpie."

"Okay. Whatever."

"Well then, since we're getting into all this, what's up with you and Bennett."

"What the hell are you talking about, what's up with me and Bennett? Nothin's up with me and Bennett."

"Bull—shit. Tell me another one."

I almost knock over my glass of beer, and while preventing that spillage almost topple the pitcher over the small tabletop. "What the hell gives you that idea?"

"What. Ever." She's smiling, giving me one of those sign language for dummies signs. The big W.

"Am I missing something here? Do you know something I don't, Nat?"

"I was merely commenting on the fact that you two seem like new secret bosom buddies, is all." Suddenly the table gets real quiet, and I'm just holding my breath, waiting for wave two of her attack. "He's hot, eh? Real hot." And she shrugs and looks innocent as she tells me, "I'd do him."

"I was fucking SICK, Nat." She doesn't seem to get this, so I say, "He's my brothers' best friend, Nathalie."

"When did that ever matter? He's a Leo, you know. You two would be perfect together."

"Great. I'll have to keep that in mind." Fact is, I already knew Zach was a Leo. I know a lot about Zach that I won't admit to, including that there's something going on between us. But I can't keep my mind on Zach. I'm too busy worrying about PK.

I keep coming back to this second when the two of us were walking back from Benny's party, and it was already dawn. The pavement glittered under the early orange sun, and we were just strolling along, holding hands. Sometimes we do that, especially when we're stoned. PK was wondering a million odd questions out loud, like: what comes after the existential dilemma?

All the sudden there was this woman in Nike running shoes and those old lady shorts rolling her baby out of a cafe we passed. She's got a huge styrofoam cup in one hand, a whopping baby carriage in the other, and she's trying to get out the door without all hell breaking loose. So Peek jumps over and holds the door open for her. She glances up through these perfectly straight-cut bangs and gives us both a quick once over. Like she's wondering what the hell vampires like us are doing hanging out in the early sunlight. Like she's worried we're going to rob her and rape and pillage her baby. She doesn't even say thank you, just hippity-hops it away, her baby all the while sleeping under these incredibly soft look-ing blue blankets.

Peek lets go of the door and it slowly expels its breath, winds back on its hinges. He's got this look on him, a really fucking sad look in his eyes that look grey when he's this tired, this sad. And I'm pretty sure it's not just because this lady thinks we're robbers and murderers—we're used to that. I'm thinking maybe I bummed him out with all my nightmare paranoia. But I watch him, watching her walk away, and then it hits me. He's staring at the baby carriage. He's staring at the baby.

"Nat," I say, "do you ever think of having kids?"

She looks dumbfounded. Her lips drop into a frown. "You

ain't preggers, are you?"

"God no. That requires sex, doesn't it?"

"Whew." She wipes her perfectly drawn eyebrow. "Yeah, of course I think about it sometimes. I think it would be cool to have this kid and dress it up in leather baby pants and fake fur and cool shit. It would be a funky kid, eh? But I don't want to be a barmaid mom. And I don't think I could hack being a lawyer's wife slash mom either, y'know?"

"What are you going to do with the rest of your life?"

She smiles a little. A secret smile. Men all around us start opening their wallets and calling over Nat's waiter friend with the crush to buy us another round. "Is this a public service poll," she asks.

"Yeah," I smile.

"Okay." A pitcher of beer lands magically on our table. Nat pours us some and raises her glasses to all the people on the patio and then clinks her glass to mine. "Okay. Well, I was thinking maybe I'd save up and go to night school or something. Maybe get into advertising or work at a travel agency or something. But the money wouldn't be nearly as good as the club, right? That's the dilemma."

"You wouldn't bartend forever though, right?"

"Naw. I think they pretty much kick your ass out of there when your boobs start to sag or you turn forty—whichever comes first." She gets this dreamy expression on her face as she takes another sip of beer. "I'd like the travel agency thing. I'd like to travel. Meet some rich Italian lord or some shit and start having his gorgeous brats. Have lots of annoying dogs that shit all over the place and have a person specially designated to clean up after them. 'Course, the dogs would bite this poor sucker all the time."

"That's a sick fantasy."

"You think that's sick you should try being on the receiving end of one of Benny's passes." She starts to giggle. Soft at first, then hard and heavy. She's spitting up beer, she's laughing so hard.

When I get to the door of PK's apartment it's like a million cracks are threatening to split my back. My cheeks feel as though they've been stuffed with cotton and then covered in cement. Like I've just spend three days in a dentist's chair and all I have to show for it is this lousy hangover. I'm just standing there in front of it, glaring at the chipped red paint, wishing Nat and I hadn't got so many free rounds. I don't want to knock. It's like I already know.

It was after hooking up with PK yesterday that acute paranoia set in, when it started to feel like the ship was going down whether I signalled for help or not. But I have to know for sure. My hair's standing up on end, prickling the back of my neck. I've got goosepimples on top of goosepimples, and it's around 25 degrees but I'm rubbing my arms like I'm cold. Finally I pull out a cigarette, light it, and start knocking.

The neighbourhood park was a riot of colour. Graffitied benches, sidewalks. The dinky fountain near the thickly painted swing set where Peek's and my initials are branded in manic panic blue. And I was staring at him, trying to figure out when things became so hideously fucked up.

Peek was rubbing his head furiously. He rubbed and rubbed and scratched.

I said, "What, you got lice or something?" He scowled at me. "What? What'd I say?"

"Leave me alone. I'm itchy."

"Maybe you should wash your hair."

"Water's been turned off again."

"Why didn't you tell me? How long?"

"Day before yesterday. Something about the plumbing downstairs. Mr. Sing needs the water for his flowers."

"Newsflash, Peek. He's not allowed to turn your water off for some fucking vegetation."

"Newsflash, Magpie. I'm not allowed to live there and work under the table. I'm not even supposed to be able to go to school."

"Whoa there. Wanna come over to my place and fight with my brothers for a shower?"

"Wouldn't want to put you out."

"It's eighty friggin' degrees out. And frankly, you're getting a little rank."

"You've convinced me," he said, jumping up from the warm sand where our feet had been stretched out. "Hey," Peek dusted off and looked around. "Notice anything different around here lately?"

"Uhm. Noo..."

"Needles. There aren't any needles here today."

"Hmm," I glanced around, appreciating, for a moment, the lack of syringes that usually dot the sand and surrounding grass.

"No condoms. No broken beer bottles..."

"Interesting. Guess that new needle depot's working, huh?"

"Humph. More likely some yuppie wants to build a condo nearby so the city sent over some goons to pick up the trash. Or it's getting to be election time."

"My, my, Peckoria. You're awfully cynical today."

PK scratched his head some more, looked away across the narrow park.

"What the hell, Peek? Except for when you *freaked* on me the other night you've given me nothing but three-word answers for the past week already. Did I do something?" And

I knew it had something to do with the night of Benny's party, or maybe that day. He'd been an asshole ever since, and I'd been downright bothered by it all.

"Naaah, Mags. Just thinkin'. Busy thinkin'."

"You're always busy thinking. What's so different about today."

"Just stuff."

"Oh my God!" I had to scream. "This is not my beautiful friend," I said to a stunted little tree.

"Come on, Mags, settle down." He paced around in nervous circles. I'd only ever seen him this quiet, this disturbed, once before. It was when he left his home and came to my place. The day his parents chucked him. For three days he paced around my bedroom like the building was on fire.

"PK."

"Mags," he said sarcastically. I felt my face heat up with the first twinges of real anger, and I was thinking, when was the last time I was actually mad at Peek? But he knows me like the back of his ass and so he said, "Alright, alright." I could hear him letting go of his breath, and it was heavy. It had weight. "I'm just getting so fucking sick of all this. I'm so tired, Mags."

"Tired of what? Like you're not getting enough sleep or Vitamin C and soap and water or what?" We set off for my house at a fairly good pace, and I had to fight to keep up with PK's long-legged strides.

"You know what I'm tired of?"

"What?" I said, trying to humour him.

"Every time I leave my apartment there's a dog or three parked outside. And then I walk down the street and there are more people walking their goddamn dogs."

"Your point being what? You hate dogs now?"

"Those dogs live better than I do. They're treated better,

eat better... fucking dogs. People glare at me if I try to move past the goddamn dog brigade that's right in front of my fucking *door*, Mags. I—I mean we—count less than them."

"Yeah, but—"

"No nonono. It's like there's this big bushel of apples, right? And this other person with a dog, they've got a bushel too. Only, the thing is, every apple I bite into is bitter and full of worms. And the other person, the guy with the dog, right? Every apple in front of him is sweet and tasty. And he has me arrested because all of my apples are bad. He's so busy scoffing at me he doesn't even see that his dog starts to eat all of my rotten, shitty apples. Naw—he *does* notice it, and that's why he's scoffing."

"That is so fucked up, PK."

"Exactly my point. I ain't gonna stand around and be that person anymore."

"And what'll you be instead? A fine, rich, upstanding member of society?"

"Shut up, Magpie," he glared at me.

"Fuck you." And of course we stopped to hold our noses, because we'd reached my dingy lobby with it's constant stench of piss and vinegar and rotting cooked fish. I started to get his point.

"I'll just be a second," I said to PK's back. "Getting you a towel."

"Thanks." He was standing in my bedroom, looking around like he'd never been there before. I could get into that because I've often looked at the apartment, my bedroom, the same way. The walls stained and dented from things my brothers threw at me, things I threw back. Ashes on the floor, a permanent dust collection rimming the narrow mattress on the floor that doubles as my bed. Windows almost rusty with age, the ceiling with its long tinsel streaks of leakage. Posters trying to disguise all this lack of love. When I came back PK was standing in front of my map of Europe, one of those full colour deals that you can get at cheap book stores. He was running his fingers across it's lines, tracing borders or rivers or mountain ranges. He didn't even notice that I was in the room.

"Peek?"

He turned, doing this slow head swivel. Like he was dreaming and I was only half a hallucination. Like he saw right past me into something else. Into a huge, three-dimensional map that filled up the room. It was fucking eerie.

"Where would you go?" he said then.

"I dunno. Anywhere, I guess." He nodded at this, as if I'd said something smart. "Here's your towel."

"I suppose," he said, taking the ratty, bleached and stained towel from me, "it doesn't matter where. I suppose it's the moving that counts. Movement. The opposite of stagnation."

"Long distance runners, right?" I smiled, trying to see the old Peekster glimmer through.

"Yeah," he said, but he looked like he wanted to cry.

"Where would you go, Peek?"

"Wherever I could."

So three cigarettes and a hairball coughing fit later I'm still knocking at his door. Maybe it's because I've been slipping into a booze coma since hanging with Nat that I barely notice how obnoxious I'm being. I suppose I've felt it coming, and I don't know why the hell I didn't say something, do something.

And I'm thinking of PK's apples, glaring at a dog that someone's tied to his doorknob right in front of me. I can practically taste the bitterness, and I've got to swallow hard. I don't know what to do, where to go now. I'm fucking freezing.

He's not at home. Who the hell knows where he actually is.

Pierced

It's Zach's birthday party, held at the same old same old, but I'm far from feeling festive. Zach smiles at me and I pretend to return it. Nat, Derek, Spanky, Benny—they're all here. My brothers shove beer under my nose, which I drink without even looking at the glass.

PK isn't at the club. I figured he would show up here. I can't concentrate on anything that's going on. I picture him standing up in the same booth where we're sitting, delivering the rules of the club, and what came after. This curling knot of dread settles in my chest and I reach for my beer. So it's true—he's really fucked off.

"Where's PK?" Everyone asks this of me at least once every hour.

I dunno. Maybe he's on his way. Maybe he ran into his parents and they actually spoke to him. I don't KNOW where PK is. He's not at Livin' Easy. I asked Mr. Sing. Maybe he came across a drug deal and got jumped. Something behind my eyes snaps.

"Zach," I yell across the table. "Whaddaya want for your birthday?"

"A Porsche," he hollers back. Everyone guffaws.

"No, really."

"I want a Porsche. It's my birthday. I can wish for anything I want." More laughter. Benny's practically rolling under the table and it's making me sick. I don't know what to do with myself, other than drink myself under the table. I can't bear to tell anyone what I suspect, but I also can't stand to see everyone having such good times.

"I'll work on that one for you," I tell Zach.

Roddy goes, "Don't you need a driver's license or something?"

Pete ducks his head in close to mine. "That's a hell of a lot of tricks you'd have to pull, Magpie. Better think it over."

"Fuck off, neanderthal." He makes kissy faces at me and Benny rolls further under the formica. And then Cat walks up, all casual like. She's dressed in some leather vest thing with a tiny undershirt, short leather skirt that shows off her new fuck-me boots and long legs. If she hiccuped you'd see a thousand leagues under the sea. She drapes her spindly arms around Zach and Pete.

"What's the occasion, fellers?" She talks to them like they're the only people in the room.

"Zach's b-day," Pete yells.

"Oh really? Why wasn't I invited? Happy birthday, Zach," she squeals and sits in his lap, her nose crinkling up, probably thinking to herself how cute she is. I long to see PK, to have someone to barf with. She leans over. It's almost like slow motion as she plants one on Zach. And I mean she really plants one. I can almost see tonsils being swapped. I can't stand to watch anymore.

"Hey Nat," I yell over to her, ignoring the scene beside me. "I love this song, don't you?"

"Sure as hell do." She grins and gets up, hitting Derek on her left who holds her fluffy dyed green ballerina skirt to make her stay. We hit the dance floor with a mission. I feel eyes watching me, wondering what the hell is up with my attitude.

After the third song of absolute thrash and grind, I calm down enough to let Nat stop me and talk to me. "Men," she says, all confidential. "Fuckin' men become stupid fucks when any woman who's marginally attractive sticks her ass in their face. No contest. He couldn't help it even if he wanted to."

"Who the fuck cares?" I say.

"Chill, Magpie. Chill, babe. It's just me here." She backs up a step. "Don't have to bite my head off."

"I'm not, really," I say, feeling like a complete asshole. I try to grab her hands, make her stay on the floor with me.

She shakes her head slightly and gives me a bored look. "I'm gonna sit this one out. Have fun."

But I can't—I give up halfway through the next song and throw myself into the crowds at the far end of the club, the other side from our booth, towards the washroom. I take my time, fluffing up my blue-do, stretching my knee-high socks up past my knee, arranging the rips in my collar, when Cat strolls in with a feline look in her eyes. She's dragged a zombie girl in with her, blond dreads obscuring her stoned face.

"Check it, girl," she says so everyone can hear. "Got a new one today. It's driving me mad. Fuckin' turn on, girl. I'm *sooo* addicted."

"What're you goin' on about, bitch." A dyed-black hardcore chick climbs out of working stall number one, spreads her hands on her black-jeaned hips.

"New piercing, man." Cat's looking right at me as she pulls her skirt up past her belly, lowers skimpy underwear to her knees. "Oh my god, I think I could come right now," she grins. Pulls on her hairless snatch and opens it up for all to see. A shiny row of metal rings glisten inside like ridiculous engagement rings or bathtub plugs. I see three, watching even though I'm disgusted, then another closer to her clit that she fiddles with. Her hands move slightly and I see more rings roving up the left side of her labia. Three more defencelessly nestling there. Gorge rises in my throat, and I push my way out through the throng gathering to ooh and aaah over her bravery. I wish I knew I could take her. I'd give her a solid knee to that metallic groin of hers.

"Hey, where the hell have you been?" Joe asks when I've finally settled my stomach enough to sit down again.

"Bathroom. Holy shit, Nat, do you know what she was doing in there?"

"Uhm. Giving the hockey team a blow job?"

"Good guess," I say, arching an approving eyebrow at her. "Showing off her latest in a large number of clit piercings to all the girls. Fucking gross."

"Oh God. Okay, I'll bite. How many?"

"Fucking seven, at least."

"Shit," Nat starts to choke on her beer, laughing. "Shit."

Spanky's sitting close by, listening. "That's not dangerous, is it?" He's got this slightly confused, worried look hovering around his lips.

"I'd say. What do you say, Nat?"

"Capital E," she says. And when Spanky looks even more lost she nods to him like a stern teacher. "For Yeast-E girl. Bet she's shaved clean as a newborn, too."

"Yup."

"What?" Spanky's eyes start to look like spinning pennies. "I didn't know you could do that."

Nat laughs all the more, so hard she's practically choking. "Listen, Spanky," she drapes her arm over his shoulder, still chuckling, "Cat is not like other girls. She's a very scary girl."

"Where the hell have you been, Magpie? I've been looking for you." It's Zach. I look up to see his face flushing six shades of scarlet. Nat starts laughing all over again.

"Why?"

"Why what?"

"Why were you looking for me," I say all cold. "Where the hell is the fire?" He backs up a bit. A little perplexed by the look of things.

"I was worried," he tells me. "Thought maybe you'd gotten sick again. Joe and Pete and I were worried about you. You took off so suddenly."

"Well don't. Don't worry about me. I'm just fine." I can tell I'm pushing the line, so I add, "Besides, it's your birthday.

You're supposed to enjoy the hell out of yourself and let us worry about you."

"Don't get cute with me, Mary Margaret."

I swear I can hear the jaws hitting the table. "Mary Margaret?" Nat snorts. Zach stands there, hands on hips, eyes flashing. I go, "What? What'd I do?"

He grabs my hand and pulls me off the seat. I see Nat grinning at me as I'm led away from the table, to the back of the club where it's quieter.

When he's stopped he drops my arm and says, "Okay, Magpie. Spill it. What's with the attitude?"

"I don't have any—" He just looks madder. "Why is everyone so mad at me these days?"

"Are you upset because PK's not here?"

"Yes," I burst out.

"What else?"

"Why does there have to be something else?"

"Because I've known you since you were practically in diapers, brat. I probably know you better than your own brothers."

"Incest is best," I chirp. He gets this expression on his face, something I've never seen before, and backs me into the wall. It's the kind of face that makes me think of exploding tin cans. I can smell booze on him, coming out of the pores of his skin.

"Why are you acting like this?"

"Like what?"

"Come on."

"No, really, tell me. Like what?"

He takes a while to answer this one. His head drops and his arms slacken. He's pulling the whole 'hurt' routine. "Y'know, I thought we were actually friends or something."

"What do you need a friend like me for when you've got Cat? Just go into the bathroom. She's just dying to be your friend."

"Cat? This is about fucking Cat?"

"Bear in mind that you're the one who said 'fucking'."

"Grow the fuck up. If you can't figure out yet that I didn't exactly invite that then you're more of a fucking baby than I thought. And I don't want to be friends with a baby."

"Whoa. I didn't ask to be your friend."

"No. You didn't. Stupid, isn't it." He's walking away and I'm thinking, what's with the melodrama? For a second I think I actually hate Zach Bennett. I mean, what a moron thing to say.

I can't help myself. I go, "What's your problem, Bennett?" and grab his shirt over the shoulder. There's a faint ripping sound. We both hear it. He stops dead in his tracks, turns around. Looks at his shoulder. Then at me, and I'm gaping at my own dumb luck. "Oh, man, sorry," I say, backing up.

"What the fuck's my problem? What the fuck's your problem?" Slowly edging towards me, just like in a crappy movie. His shadow looms over me and I cringe, thinking, wow, things can turn on a dime. "Who do you think you are? You little baby. You jealous little snit."

Have to hand it to him. He knows all of my buttons and how to push them. "I ain't jealous, you fucking clod." And suddenly I'm like someone else, someone I hate. I push him, yelling, "I don't have to watch old men having sex with sluts in front of me is all."

"Listen," he grabs my arms with one hand, and my chin in the other. I'm so pissed I'm seeing red and there's sweat trickling down my forehead. I've got my eyes closed, still waiting for the blows to come. While I'm waiting there's this moment, like everything's trapped in a single line of a song. It's like a big giant soap bubble where I'm just thinking about all the shit that's been happening lately. I mean, really. It's too much.

"Listen." I open my eyes again and he's staring at me with this queer expression on his lips. Almost a smile. "I'd rather rot in hell than touch her and you know it." He leans down then, the shadow of his head swooping down on me. I feel a light caress across my lips before he lights out again. "'Sides," he laughs, backing away from me, "I'm into young girls that I can pervert." I try to hit him again but he's out of range. Feeling about twelve years old again, and I'd love to disappear I feel so stupid.

—

Cleo's Cue

The days pass like some kind of bad dream. Me and my faithful sidekick Spanky sit down to rest on the sidewalk somewhere near the Bull. The streets smell like sweaty socks after a night of dancing. Traffic stalls and pushes forward on invisible strings. We've been gawked at, glared at, almost spat at. All because we're sitting down. On the street. People are really getting their rocks off thinking that we're going to ask them for change, their faces screwing up into a miserable knot. Sometimes I think about doing it just for fun. But then Spanky's just sitting there, not asking for dick all, and this dude in a suit drops money into Spanky's palm like this guy's just been waiting to unload his damned change.

"Shit, we must look bad."

He's looking at his fist that's now holding a looney and a few shiny dimes. Says, "Maybe they think I'm a leper."

"Isn't that the disease where your nose and dick fall off?"

"I dunno." A few minutes go by maybe, and I'm busy being pissed off about the suit who thinks that every kid with blue hair is trying to rip him off. I mean I'm really enjoying this fume, and then Spanky goes, "Where you think he's gone?"

PK. We're looking for PK.

"Magpie?" My throat's busy being all clogged, so I don't say anything. "Don't think he's the type for drugs. Just don't see that. And anyway I thought everyone runs away *to* the city, not *from* it."

No. Not drugs. That's not PK's trip. He's just gone off to find stuff. That's all. He's not the type to bite it with a honking needle in his arm. He's not the type to sniff glue or some shit. So where the hell did he go? Good fucking question, I think. "I think—ahum—I think that maybe we won't find him around here."

"Yeah. Kinda thought so," Spanky says. "Buy you a coffee? Got all this money."

I try to laugh but it comes out all loud and inappropriate. "You sure you want to spend that all in one place?" It hits me then. This giant wave just about knocks me on my ass, and I don't know what to do with it. It's the guy who gave Spanky change, and all the people who didn't. And it's PK being gone, the kid in front of the Underground. It's everything, and its eating me up. I'm just about on the edge, so I go, "Spanky? How can you wake up every day and tie up your shoe laces and move on and put up with all this *shit*?"

Spanky pulls Cleo out of his coat and strokes her back. He's just sitting there like your average 15-year-old street guru, thinking. Across the street a bunch of punks are pulling their operation. I see this guy with wicked tattoos hork and spit, light a home-rolled cig.

I'm, just sitting there, fuming, and Spanky's shaking his head. "What? What already," I say.

"Wrong question."

"Okay. So what's the right question?" For a fraction of a second I'm so interested that I actually forget about PK. I even forget to feel so frigging awful.

"How come those kids—" Spanky says, pointing to the punks, who are begging for change at the corners. There's this car full of 'Burbanites stopped at the corner, and they're all rolling up their car windows like they're about to be car-jacked. I mean *really*. It's 30 degrees out. And Spanky goes, "—Really *scare* people? What's so scary about those kids? What's so offensive about them? Huh?" Nickels and dimes and a lone shiny loonie gleam in his palm.

"Yeah," I say.

He's all defiant now. "There's no way back in, that's all I see. The wheels are turning without me, that's for sure. They're too scared to let me back in. Or them," he points back to the punks.

I pull my finger across Cleo, feeling the tiny fur bristle. "Can I tell you something, Spanky?"

"Sure you can."

I have this overwhelming urge to tell Spanky everything. I mean really blurt it out, all the gory details. I don't know, though. Somehow it doesn't seem appropriate right now. It's like I can't even get into the cardboard box that holds that particular brutal time. That's definitely one of my double-taped memories. Something's on the tip of my tongue anyway, so I go, "I don't think he'll come back for a while." But I also want to give Spanky a little lift. "I thought for sure he was gone once before," I say. "He got kicked out of his place. It was only for a few hours, y'know?—That he was missing, I mean. But I was worried as hell about him."

I don't—can't—tell Spanky what I'm really thinking. I don't say a word about that awful day, when it seemed like the end of the world. I won't tell him about Jessie and her closet. I don't tell him about my nightmares, or hers. It's there, though, waiting for me. It'll get me when I'm sleeping, I'm sure, but for now it's not coming out.

Maybe I don't want to say anything because Spanky looks completely bagged out. "Have you been sleeping?"

"Nah. Derek's mom got tired of me crashing. Guess it was bad for business. She was afraid it was going to be a habit, so he had to say adios." He rubs at his eyes with a grimy fist. "Got to admit, Magpie. Gettin' real fed up with all this."

It's like I'm hearing PK's voice coming back from wherever, fitted into Spanky's mouth. Shockwaves are going up and down my arms. "Jesus, Spanky. Why didn't you tell me?"

"It's survivable."

It's all getting to be a bit much.

In a flash it's morning and I'm exhausted, spent like my last dollar. Crisp new air is coming into my nostrils through the open window, wiping out the ripe smell of garbage covered in wasps. Early morning August. The walls of my room look rosy, as though someone's throwing a barbeque bash in the sky. And I'm thinking, so this is what it means to be in decline.

The night before comes back to me in waves. The table overturned inside the dark cave of the bar, knocked over by Benny's fucked-up body. Beer scent drifting over the room, locked inside a smoky belly and haze of faces. A joint—and I kid you not— called Satan's Brew.

Conversation going something like this. I think of PK's dogs and say: Fuuuck, d'ya think we've got bad karma? I mean, who the hell came up with all this shit? *Derek:* We created it. All of it. *Nathalie to Derek:* Yours is created, honey. The rest of ours is inherited. *Derek to Nathalie:* Can't you ever be serious? *Nathalie to Derek:* Why the hell should I want to be serious? Too fucking depressing. *Me to Nathalie:* What are you afraid of, Nat? *Nathalie:* Reality.

The word is out that PK's really gone. I mean, everybody knew. They just didn't want to believe it. PK stories pass across the small round tables. *Benny:* He'll be back. They always come back. Unless they're dead.

Grime under my fingernails, pushed in further from me scratching at the table. Everything spinning. Could be the shrooms, or maybe the beer and tequila. Everything melting inward, my hands suddenly stretching. The table's slick, like the wood's been bawling, glistening with spilt pitchers.

Spanky: Maybe it's more like, what are we gonna do about it?

Benny: Yeah, man, that's it. Fuck, but you know we have a right to bitch, man.

Nathalie: How's that, Benny? You ever tried working for a living?

Benny: Aw, don't be a bitch, Nat.

Nathalie: Fuck you, Benny. What've you ever done besides sell drugs and small-time hood shit?

On Benny—a grin so wide it swallows half the air left in the room. *Benny to Nat:* Why the hell do you think that's my fucking occ-u-pa-tion? I don't want to turn out like you, Nat. Fucking busting tables for dick while some fat bastard grabs my tits and stuffs bills down my bra. I'd rather be your pimp, ho. Cleaner hands.

Derek hoots, brings his hand down on the table. Nat's jaw drops. She tries not to laugh.

Benny: Now, I'm not saying that what you do ain't legit business, Nat, getting by on your ass and all. Hell, ain't that the oldest profession on earth? But what I do is just as legit. What do you want me to do, go to school or some shit? What am I gonna do? Come on. Think about it. Am I gonna go to work making six bucks an hour cleaning toilets, get by on fucking two-dollar Mardi Gras cheques when I'm laid off? No. I'm gonna sell drugs to rich motherfuckers who've always been rich so that I can afford a nice little life of my own.

Nat: And when that doesn't work out you'll suck their fat, rich dicks, right Benny? Oldest profession on earth.

Derek roars with laughter. And the room is dim, and it's only getting dimmer. A blanket of emptiness floats on top of everything. Me thinking—this is no way to live. Plaster is falling off the walls in thick, curly handfuls. Walls that look like the outside of a glass of cold beer—shiny with condensation. Permanent stench of beer and sweat, a layer of grease that drips from every air molecule. Naked light bulbs strung between Christmas lights shrouded by a curling curtain of smoke. And then Spanky turns to us again, rubbing away at his eyes with a fist never quite clean. He's suddenly revolting, kind of pathetic and no one you want to hold close.

Spanky: Y'know, I'm so sick of this. All I hear you guys do is bitch bitch bitch. DO something.

Derek: What do you want us to do, tough guy?

Spanky: I dunno. Something. Get a job. Start a revolution.

Derek: I had a job once. I *was* that asshole cleaning toilets. I cleaned office buildings with my mother. Then I had another job. I parked fucking cars. You know what?

Spanky: What?

Derek: I got to admit my mother's on to something. I'd rather suck a real dick than pretend that I'm not doing it at those shitty jobs.

Me: Whazza matter, Spanky. Wazz wrong?

And there's something wrong with all of it, though I couldn't give it a name. But if I were to guess it would be a little like the day you realize you're poor. Or the day you realize that the rest of your life is going to be one miserable flash after another. Only maybe this is Spanky's first taste. Maybe the rest of us had it lucky—it hit us earlier, and now it only comes back like the ride coming to a stop every now and then. Like when something bad happens to one of our own. And there's a catch to Spanky's voice that I just can't bear to listen to:

Spanky: I'm just so sick of it. I don't know what to do. Every time I reach for something it fucks up, it changes into something else, something that's falling down. It's a fucking house of cards.

Spanky's face scrunches like he's been punched in the gut. He reaches inside his bottle-green jacket. Serious b.o. wafts out from his coat, that unwashed ripe smell of the street, like old fries and garbage. He releases Cleo from his sleeve onto the stool beside him, unfurling her like he's throwing dice.

She scampers down the legs and onto the floor—into the throng of leather-clad patrons, into Satan's Brew, towards any dark hole, to hide and cower in the dark.

Jessie's
Brand New Closet

So instead of nursing my hangover with hair of the dog I wake up and slide back into my knee-length cut-offs and a dirty t-shirt and actually make it to the door when Spanky's on time. I don't even feel like throwing up, so I figure I couldn't have been all that drunk. He's wearing a hangdog expression, and I'm thinking maybe he remembers throwing up on the paper box on our way out of the club.

I sit him down for a cup of coffee and he goes, "What're we doing today?"

"Uh, I dunno. Man, does my head hurt. I think there's something in that damned beer."

"Where are we going to look today? East side? We haven't really done that yet."

"—Maybe it's some chemical or some shit. I read about that stuff. All these preservatives like—"

"I meant PK. Where are we looking for PK today?"

I'm smoking a cigarette. I mean I'm really smoking that bastard, inhaling it like it's some sort of lifeline. I have no idea I'm so tense and upset until I sort of step outside myself and see it. Me. Acting all fucked up and abandoned, and trying to play it cool. I mean, I don't even know why I'm avoiding Spanky's question, simple as it is. PK's been gone for a few weeks now, maybe a month, and I'm still walking around like a zombie on crack. It's starting to get real tired, is what I'm thinking.

I force myself to concentrate on what Spanky just said until suddenly it's like I'm hearing a bell go off in my head. If PK were skipping town, he'd want to clear up some unfinished business, wouldn't he? Even if he didn't want to do it with me. And aside from his parents, who I'm sure he doesn't want to deal with, I can only think of one person PK would want to see. When inspiration hits it's no small thing, so I tell Spanky, "Uhm, yeah, the east side. I thought we'd stop in and visit this old friend of ours—I mean, a friend of me and Peek's. You game?"

"Sure," he shrugs, and pushes a long greasy lock out of his eyes.

He looks suspiciously well rested for once. I give him the old arched eyebrow. "Where'd you sleep last night?"

"Hm. Well, Derek snuck me in to his room. I slept on the floor in his closet, so his mom wouldn't come in and find out. Can't do it too often, though. Don't wanna get Deke kicked out, y'know?"

Coincidence or not, I take this to be a sign. Kind of like a boulder dropped in your lap. "Jesus H. on a pogo stick, Spanks. Sounds like kismet to me."

"Uh, Mags? You need some food or something?"

"Yeah—no. I mean, I have a clue for once. Let's skedaddle."

"I have no idea what you're talking about."

"Long story, Spanks."

This one day Peek and I found out what happened to her—to Jessie. It was only about a year ago, I guess. We were going along the street, just hanging out, when we bumped into Jessie's mother. It must have been habit—we dropped and crushed our cigarettes. She saw anyway, and when she finally came face-to-face with us she looked pretty annoyed. "Mrs. Belson," PK said. "Uhm, hi!" I said. I've got to give her credit, she recovered pretty quick.

"Well, hello," she said, and smoothed a wave of hair behind her ear. It's funny, that one movement really changed her. I mean, she looked older. There were lines around her eyes. I could even see some white hair mixed in with the blonde. But she also still looked really young. It's amazing how some people can look that way—young and old all at once. Like a little girl, all sweet and nervous, pushing her hair back.

We were all a little tongue-tied. We hadn't heard from Jessie since the day the three of us had the wind knocked out of our sails. I didn't even know how to begin. But apparently Mrs. Belson knew more about these things than we did.

"Jessica will be delighted that I ran into you both."

"How's she doing? We haven't heard hide nor hair of her," PK said like Jess had been off on a ritzy cruise or something. He's always been really good with grownups.

"She's good. She likes her new school."

"Good, good," PK frowned and then I just couldn't stop myself. I opened my big fat mouth and dove in.

"Mrs. Belson—I mean—I'm really sorry I just left like that but there was a situation—"

Mrs. Belson waved a gorgeous slender hand at me like she was directing traffic. "It was a long time ago. Besides, it hadn't anything to do with you," her mouth said, but her eyes flashed like she knew I'd personally demonized her daughter. Sometimes I wondered if Jessie's mom is the reason why we haven't heard from her. I didn't know what PK was thinking, but I was shuffling my boots, wondering why the hell we didn't pretend that Mrs. Belson never crossed our path. "I know she'd like to hear from you both," she said, and then I felt like the doe caught in the proverbial headlights. She pulled out this pad of paper from her wallet, a pen, started scribbling something down. When she ripped the paper off, it sounded like the roar of an engine.

"Anyway, here's our address and phone number. I'm sure you remember that we moved." Mrs. Belson tried to give us a smile, but it came out like a wince. The whole scene cast this strange pall over the day, made us shiver all the more when it started raining. When Mrs. Belson walked by us I turned and watched her, seeing, for a second, a glimpse of Jess's walk. I don't know. It kind of felt like being haunted.

So me and Spanky are off, walking towards the address in a way upscale part of town. It's not such a long hitch at all, and I can't believe I didn't think of it before. Frankly, the idea of visiting Jessie feels like jumping off a cliff. But it's for PK, I remind myself, it's for Peek.

All the sudden we're standing at the door and the bell's ringing like some goddamned wind chime. I'm so out of it I didn't even think to call first. Mrs. Belson answers the door and her mouth gapes open and closed for a minute before she recognizes me and gets a hold of herself. But in those seconds she's looking us up and down I can see us through her eyes. I know we look bad. Safety pins sticking out of everything, holes all over like we've been sleeping in a den of moths. My hair all electric and flailing and Spanky's soft, spotty skin. No doubt we also reek. I've been drunk for two days and haven't bathed in about three. God only knows about Spanky. But I look pretty serious, as I often do when I'm so seriously hung over.

It's like I'm possessed by Peek's mouth for a moment. I go: "Hello, Mrs. Belson. This is my friend Spanky. We were wondering if we could visit Jessie."

And Mrs. Belson goes, "Magpie, what a surprise. Would you two like to come in and have some tea?"

"Uhm. Sure."

So we walk in to this huge house, and Mrs. Belson's yelling at the stairway, "Jessie, Magpie's here to see you," and flipping back a wave of her blond hair.

So we're seated in the livingroom, and Mrs. B is pulling out some cookies and tea for us. It's all cozy and nice—a real nice house. Everything looks like it's straight from an IKEA catalogue, all these space age lamps and stuff. There's an expensive-looking carpet on the floor and a garden out back that I can see from a set of patio doors.

"Well, what a pleasant surprise," Mrs. Belson says.

Spanky just gives her this beatific smile through a mouth full of cookie crumbs. It's like he's never had a cookie before, the way he's gorging on it. But I have to say, bad table manners aside, he doesn't look the least out of place in a joint like this. Me, though, I'm all fidgety. I've never been in a house this big. Or this nice. I'm afraid that my feet stink, that my socks are so dirty they'll leave permanent streaks on the Belsons' nice rug.

Jessie's mom suddenly gets this irritated look on her face. For a second I think she's discovered my feet smell and is grossed out, but then she gets up and over to the staircase again. "Jessica! I don't want to have to call you again." I think she's going to climb up the stairs and fetch Jess, but then she turns back and looks at us again, smiling a little, and sits down.

"So how's school going for you, Mary Margaret?"

Spanky looks like he's about to spit his cookies out, so I go, "Oh, I made the honour roll again this year, Mrs. Belson. Me and PK both."

"Excellent. That's just great to hear. And do you go to the same school, er—?"

"Spanky," I say.

And Spank, cookie crumbs flying everywhere, says, "Ah'm-b'tween-schools."

"Oh. Here, dear." She hands him a napkin.

And I'm thinking, did Spanky grow up in a barn? I can feel my face getting all hot so I say, "How about Jessie?"

"Well, we home-schooled her for a year or two. And now she goes to Brant. I think she enjoys it." Mrs. Belson flashes us a mouth full of perfect teeth. But it's all fake. I'm getting hot under the collar. I mean, Brant. How the hell can Jessie stand a place like Brant? That's a jetsetter school where all the kids drive expensive cars and holiday in the fucking

Bahamas or some shit. Definitely a Buffy, Muffy and Biff kind of school.

For the first time it occurs to me that maybe everything's different now. Maybe the Belsons have gone so far up in the world that people like us can't even sit in the livingroom and talk. And just when I'm thinking this I notice a gigantic hole in my sock where my big toenail, dressed in black polish, is poking through. That's when Jessie comes in the room.

It's funny to see her now. Her hair's real long and straight, carefully brushed and held back with a head band. She's my age but she could pass for about fourteen still. Very pale, her skin pearly and naked looking, like it's never seen an inch of makeup. I can't help it. She looks so beautiful, regal. Like something out of a Ralph Lauren ad.

"Magpie?"

"Jess, how the hell are you?"

"Good, good," she says. But it's the way she says it, I guess. A bad vibe starts working on me the minute I lay eyes on her and I'm pretty sure this isn't the Jessie I used to know and love. "What are you doing here?"

"Uhm. Well, I'm sorry we couldn't call or anything first. I was just wondering if you could spare us a minute."

She glues on her mom's smile, the one I can tell is more fake than fake leather, and says, "Of course." She sashays over and sits in a chair, and immediately takes in the hole in my sock.

"So how's life, Princess?" I say. And I really want to kick myself.

"Pretty good." Her head swivels up real slow, like she's coming to us from underwater TV. "Where's PK?"

"Uhm, he couldn't make it today," I say, eyeing her mom nervously. "Jess, this is my friend Spanky."

"Hi. Pleased to meetcha," he mumbles. Jessie stares at

him with these big serious eyes, holds out her hand to be shaken. He puts out his paw like he's the fucking Queen of England, and I'm suddenly annoyed as hell. And then I'm ashamed that I'm ashamed I brought Spanky, and it's all getting a little fucked up in my head. I take a deep breath, trying to remember the mission. I want to come clean but not in front of Jessie's mom. I don't know why, it just seems like a bad idea.

Just then, like some sort of miracle, Mrs. Belson smiles and says, "Excuse me. I've got to get the laundry finished."

When she finally leaves the room I go, "Uhm, well, that's sort of why I'm here. PK, I mean." And then I freeze. "How do you like the new place?" I ask, getting all conversational. Spanky shoots me a look. He's got crumbs all over his lips.

"Okay."

"Okay? That's it? Oh—kay? It looks like a fucking palace."

For once she's getting it a little. She cracks the tiniest of smiles, and I'm all pleased with myself.

"Want to come up and see my bedroom?"

"Yeah, sure. That would be great."

Spanky's eyes wander all over Jessie's room at the top of the stairs, and I get it when I finally walk in. It's bare. And I do mean bare. Why do rich people have such bare rooms? A lamp, a bed with a thin summer blanket draped over the end. A tiny closet with the door wide open. Rows of dresses hanging off these expensive looking hangers. There's a picture on the wall across from her bed. It's this funny picture with lots of strokes, one of those really bright things filled with primary colours, blue and red and yellow. It's one of those prints that I can imagine hanging in a dentist's office, somewhere where they have to cheer you up.

I go, "So what was that home school stuff like? What did they have you doing?"

She thinks about it for a minute before she answers. "It wasn't so bad. I just sat around the kitchen table all morning and did homework."

"Do you like Brant?"

"I love Brant. It's awesome."

"What do you do for fun these days?"

"Oh, the usual stuff, I guess. I see Matt a lot."

"Who's Matt?" Spanky asks.

"He's my boyfriend," she says and looks at me with these huge, solemn eyes. And I see it, all the sudden. It's cold and kind of sad. She's scared of us. She doesn't want to go back there at all, not to the place I left her. I'm thinking it was a mistake to come, this huge lump in my throat is choking me, when Jess points at Spanky and goes, "Is he your boyfriend?"

"Naw," I say. "Spanky's just a big ole' stray cat that me and PK took in. He needs his milk. Meow."

Spanky snorts, mumbles, "More like the other way around." He lifts up this fancy picture frame. It's sitting on Jessie's dresser, a shot of the whole family together when Jessie was younger. Sitting around a Christmas tree, opening presents and smiling. The kind of happy family shot that just sends chills up and down my spine. Jessie watches Spanky like a fucking hawk and I'm having some sort of hangover attack. Sweat beads and trickles down my back.

"Don't you guys have air-conditioning in this castle?" I say.

"Magpie," she says, and it's said softly but it's a command. "Where's PK? What's happened to him?"

Well here goes, I think, and pace the room a bit, worried about how she'll take this. And then I say, "Well, that's kinda why we're here, Jess. I need your help."

"Help? Okay." And she smiles up at me. But it's ugly. I mean, it's the kind of smile that psychos put on when they're drowning kittens or some shit. And I have no idea what that's about, but I can see the hair stand up on Spanky's head.

"Uhm. Well, first of all—has PK come to visit lately? I mean, this summer? By himself?"

She gives me this confused look at first, like I've suddenly thrown her for a loop. "PK?" And she shakes her head, "No, I haven't seen PK in years. Why?"

"You sure? You sure PK didn't stop by?"

"I'm quite sure I'd remember," she frowns.

"Okay. Okay." I take deep breaths, stand up, walk a circle around the tiny room, try to think. Spanky stands near the door. He looks about ready to bolt.

"What happened, Magpie," Jessie says in this really sweet voice.

I stop in front of her. I don't know what else to do. I can't just leave her worrying about what *might* have happened. So I look her straight in the eyes. And I say, "PK took off about a month ago, Jess. I'm trying to find him."

"He's gone?"

"Yeah. I don't know," I say, "I'm sure he just needed a vacation." But I can see the wheels spinning in her head, kinda slow but all too quick in the doom department. Just like mine.

There's a long pause in the room until Jess finally says, "How long has it been?"

"Uh—I dunno. A month? Less than that? Not so long, really."

"He's gone? Just disappeared?"

"I'm just trying to find out if he's been here. That would give me a clue, see—"

Jessie's mouth opens and closes and I'm quiet, waiting to see what's coming next.

"Jess?" I say. "Jessie, talk to me."

This awful expression comes over her face. It's like I'm looking at someone else, someone who'd rather run me over than talk to me. She leans back on her bed, looking all haughty.

"So what do you want me to do about it? I suppose you want some money or something. Well, I don't have any."

"What? What did you say?" And I'm shaking my head, thinking I must have been slipped some crack or something.

"—I mean, I haven't seen or heard from you in years. And you come in looking like some two-bit street punks. What the fuck do you want? Really?"

I can feel my face turning beet red, and I hear Spanky mumbling behind me, "Uhm, I think we should go now, Mags."

"Yeah," Jessie goes, "I think it would be best if you'd just leave."

And she's sitting up now, looking all intent.

"What do I—" And I'm stammering like a loser. I can't even breathe I'm so shocked, and I can feel my hands starting to tremble, like they do before I've gotta scrap someone. "What happened to you, Jessie? What the fuck happened to you—"

"Get real. Listen, you came to me for help? All right, here's my help. If PK disappeared it's because he's trash. Just like you. Just like your smelly little street punk friend here. You're all. Just. Trash."

Spanky's hanging out at the bedroom door like he's ready to bolt and cry, and I'm still just standing there. I can hear him like he's a million miles away, talking to me through tin can string, "Let's get out of here, Mags. C'mon, let's go!"

She hates us. I mean she really *loathes* us. And all I do, all I say to her, is so stupid. It's like my mouth is on automatic pilot, and all my brain can squeeze out is this: "You're a fucked-up, fucking traitor, Jessie. I never asked you for a dime." And I'm leaning over her now, and she's all leaning back. I can hear her bed creaking slowly. She's got this look on her face like she's about to scream bloody blue murder, and it's not because she's being malicious now. She's piss-her-pants fucking scared of me. "—And I never will ask you for anything. But you better remember one thing if you're ever walking down the street at night, Jessie. I will never forget. Anything."

I storm out of the room, the house, with Spanky in tow, but it's like I can't even see anymore. I keep thinking, damn, did PK know about this? Damn, why didn't I kick her ass? And I'm suddenly back on that street corner, staring at Jessie going by on the bus. That last time I thought she was still living the nightmares, and she was sleepwalking, the world falling apart. But maybe what happened was that when she came out of it, came out of her sleepwalking, something else happened. Maybe she decided that the only way to survive was to distance herself. Maybe she figured that she was on the winning side now, and she wanted it to stay that way. So she bought into it all. All the crap. All the lies. Like we can infect her just by being in the same room. And I'm too fucked up by this little bombshell to even get all worked up about it. I feel like I'm in one of Jessie's old nightmares, a ghost, and I'm flying around looking at the scene, all detached.

And I'm wondering now if that crater she fell into in that dream she told me and PK about—I'm wondering if that crater was filled with people like me. Her version of doom has turned into—what did she call us? Two-bit street punks? Maybe she's started to believe that only rich people survive the end of the world. And who knows? Maybe she's right.

A Is For Apocalypse

Yesterday I was in this store, just looking around. I was early to meet Spanky and I wanted to kill some time. It was the kind of store that sells punk and banger paraphernalia. Metal-studded chokers and big-ass docs. I mean, this store was so old school they still had Skinny Puppy and SNFU t-shirts.

There was this row of t-shirts hanging on a rack, and I was looking through them when something caught my eye. It was a picture on a t-shirt—this really famous picture that I remember seeing before—of a man getting his brains blown out during the Vietnam war. There was a caption on the top of the print. It read: "V is for Violence."

The next one and the next one, all the way through the alphabet, had some sort of insane message on it. "W is for War," another said, and it sported a picture of Nixon grinning at a podium. There was one of a missile launching pad. I suppose it was about the Cuban Missile crisis, because the shirt read: "K is for Kennedy." And then there was another one for K, like they had so many options. A bunch of guys in white sheets burning crosses: "K is for Ku Klux Klan." "G is for Greed," showed a bunch of bums hanging out and sun-bathing in a park. "C is for Chernobyl," was about half-melted kids standing around with cancer and radiation poisoning. I was kind of struck dumb by these shirts. It was like I heard a door creaking open in my head and from out of nowhere in walks this creepy art. I mean, every single one knocked me on my ass, sent shivers up and down my spine.

Some of the shirts, I have to admit, made absolutely no sense to me. Like: "P is for Pope," this one said, and it showed John Paul waving his hands to some bowing people. I mean, where the hell is the message in that? But it was the last one in the bunch that really freaked the hell out of me. It was for the letter A. Underneath the caption there was a billowing mushroom cloud, dusty looking in the grainy black and white print, rising from nowhere and headed straight into oblivion. A blinding flashbulb lighting it up from inside, like the face of God. It read: "A is for Apocalypse."

I turned around, asked the clerk, "How much for this shirt?" I didn't want to try it on. I didn't even care if it fit.

"Seventeen."

"Ah, come on, man. Really. How much?"

I figured the clerk had to be cool—he had green hair and one of those bull piercings through his septum. He sized me up and down, checking out how tattered my boots were. I guess it was his game to figure out which kids has money and which ones didn't. Kind of like an equal opportunity sales dude. He lifted his eyebrow, asked me, "How much you got?"

I checked my pockets. I had eleven-fifty but I said, "Nine bucks."

"Okay," he said, and shrugged.

I took my new t-shirt and walked out into the street. The sun sparkled off the cars, off the glass. It was blinding. Underneath the light everything was completely surreal. I walked towards the park like an automaton, while something inside me clicked and whirred. Spanky was already waiting for me by the time I got there. He said, "So, where are we looking today?"

I couldn't help it. Ever since we visited Jessie—all summer, actually—I've been feeling like a cosmic doormat, like the whole planet's just waiting to wipe its feet on my ass. Something happened, though, when I was looking at those shirts. I kept clamping and unclamping my hand around the throat of the one I carried away with me. I said, "We aren't looking."

"Whaddaya mean? Come on, where we going?"

"PK's gone," I said. I guess it came out all flat. Kind of like how I felt. Spanky looked like I'd slapped him.

"You serious?"

"Yeah. Listen. He's gone, okay? PK is gone. We shouldn't waste any more of our time."

"Oh."

"Naw, come on, Spanky. Don't look at me like that." I didn't know why I was getting all mad. I don't even know why I didn't just tell him what I was thinking. That PK didn't want to be found. That PK had deserted me. That it all just snapped into place while I was looking at a bunch of stupid t-shirts. "I mean, really. How long have we been looking for?"

Spanky screwed up his face for a minute, like he'd been sucking on a lemon. "Don't let that wanker bitch get to you, Mags. I know she used to be your friend and all, but you can't let her win—"

"Hey, this has nothing to do with Jessie," I said. I mean, it did, but it didn't. If PK hadn't been around to see her, then he really was gone, the way I saw it. Besides, I couldn't even apologize to Spanky for that whole scene, let alone explain it. After we left Jessie's I just pretended that whole thing didn't happen. I so didn't want to go there.

"It's just that," and Spanky avoided my eyes as he said this, "I thought PK was your best friend."

"He *is* my best friend. But what the hell do you want me to do? He ain't here. And short of calling in a missing person's report—which I won't—there's nothing I can do about it."

"Oh," he said again. "So, I guess—"

"You guess what?"

"I guess we don't have to meet any more."

The way he said it, it was so sad. I mean, I looked at him. Spanky was a kid in decline. He really looked crummy. I could see it in his eyes, what it meant to him. Looking for PK, that whole routine, that being with someone day in and day out— it kept Spanky going. If I took that away from him I'd better replace it with something. And I couldn't keep looking for PK. It was eating me up, the hopelessness of it all.

So I went, "Naw. Hell, I got a better idea."

"What's that," he said.

I put my hand on his shoulder and I looked him in the eyes and I said, "How about we find you a place to live." Spanky went all misty-eyed, like I'd just been profound or some shit.

We'd hung out for like an entire day before I screwed up the balls to ask him: "So what're you gonna do, tonight, Spanks?"

"Oh, you know," he grinned, "go to London, have dinner with the Queen, I thought."

"Seriously."

"Seriously? I dunno. I thought I'd go see if Benny was home. See if he wants to hang out."

"Hey Spanky," I said, stuffing my remaining two-fifty into his fist, "watch out for Benny. Okay?"

"Why? What's going on?"

"Nothing, nothing." I didn't want to spell out my suspicions. Just in case Spanky didn't know how to keep his mouth shut. Just in case I was right. "I think he's going through some hard times, and he gets a little unstable." I shrug, "You know how people get. A transition period. That's all."

"Okay. Sure, Mags," he said, all trusting.

But when I got home I found out that Benny wasn't going to be around for Spanky to hang with. My brothers were on their way to the Sphinx where Benny was doing some bouncing that night. I shut myself in my room, thinking of Spanky sleeping in the park after wandering around hungry all day. Two-fifty won't get a person very far. I pictured him dumpster diving, panning on the corner. I was starving just thinking about him.

And I still had the shirt in my hand. It was getting grimy

from me carrying it around in my sweaty paw all day. I didn't know what to do with it. So I took some thumb tacks I had in a shoe box. I went over to my map of Europe, the one that had basically put PK into a trance, and I pinned it on top of the map. For the rest of the night I just lay on my mattress, staring at the continents drifting behind this shirt, thinking, V is for Violence. A is for Apocalypse.

So I'm still hungry from last night. I can't eat, thinking about Spanky having nothing. I feel like I'm on fire, like I've got to get something done like yesterday. But as it turns out, this is the worst possible day to talk to Fran about anything, let alone about Spanky. She sits at the kitchen table. A glass of what looks like coke and ice is in easy reach. And I go, "Mom, I gotta ask you a big favour."

"Magpie. Honey. Sit down," she says and favours me with a grey-toothed grin. But I'm not surprised when it doesn't go well. She never calls me Magpie. She's drunk, or drinking, at any rate, and it's ten-thirty in the frigging morning. "Whattcha gotta ask me, sweetie." Her mouth opens with that lurid grin and I look for bubbles on top of her head, filled with captioned words and a 'burp' at the end.

"It's about a friend of mine."

"Is that PK back yet," she asks, leaning over her drink and reaching for one of my cigarettes, and in the process she knocks over the salt shaker, spilling salt everywhere.

"Nah, but I wanted to ask you—"

"I sure do like that kid. Too bad he turned out that way—a runaway."

"He ain't a runaway, okay? Don't you remember? His parents kicked him out—like—forever ago. Anyway—"

I know I've got this childish valley girl gape on my face, but I can't seem to stop myself. My mother waves a calloused, regal hand at me. "Don't interrupt me, Mary Margaret. Now I know you kids haven't had it easy but there's no need for that behaviour. Your brothers runnin' around like hooligans. No respect." She takes a swallow of dark liquid.

"What're you drinking, Mom?"

"None of your damn business."

"Okay, cool. It's just that I can smell the rum from here," I say before I can bite down on my tongue.

"Don't you talk back to me, young lady," she roars.

"Mom, did something happen? You okay? I mean—you never do this." And that's when she crumples. Literally. Her face falls, the lines all sagging downward, and then her head falls onto her arms. A second later I realize the sounds coming from her mouth, a hoarse, rasping cough, is actually sobbing. I rub her back, feeling like a three-year-old and a hundred all rolled up in one, until she calms down a bit.

"That's it. It's all over," she finally gasps, and grabs my wrist a little too tight for comfort. "Don't tell your brother yet, eh Mary Margaret?"

"Tell them what?"

She looks down at her chapped hands, now folded up on the table around the stem of her drink, as if there was no more life left in them. "It's over. I won't be cleaning the church no more." It comes out like a balloon a week after the party, all sagging and depressed.

"Ahh—fu-pheew—did they can you?"

She takes a minute to answer, and then she says, "No one came out and said nothing directly. It's the new committee. Puritans," she spits the word out like it's dirty.

"Well," I go, "it is a church, Fran."

Now she's really letting loose. Glass raised and wagging as she talks. "Rumours, for Christ's sake. They don't like the rumours. I can't work there no more. Not as long as he is.

O'course, he's the one with the life appointment," she mocks.

"Oh," I say, and then it dawns on me what in the hell she's talking about. "Oh. Oh fuck, Mom. You're fucking kidding me!"

"I don't know what we'll do now." The tears threaten again. "We don't have savings, God help us," and she makes the sign of the cross on herself, "and Joseph and Peter and yourself, and no jobs." Snot explodes everywhere as she breaks into hysterics again. I get up, hand her a tissue. "I can't take it, Mary Margaret. Not again," she says through blowing her nose.

"Well Jesus, Mom, you probably shouldn't have been sleeping with the priest unless he was in charge of hiring and stuff—" I meant it as a joke—sort of. Her eyes, I swear. I've never seen her so pissed off. And then she pulls back her hand. I can see it coming but I guess I'm kind of in a daze. She slaps me. My head rings and I can actually see bright plinking lights float in front of my eyes.

"Don't you ever. And I mean ever. Talk to me like that again, Mary Margaret. That man was very good to us for years. You got that? He got us food when we were hungry. He helped pay the bills—God knows I couldn't have done it on my own. And he got a hell of a good position for a woman like me." Her voice gets stronger, more capable, as she yells at me. I can't believe we're actually speaking openly about it, for the first time, so many years later.

She takes another drink, and another one of my cigarettes to replace the one she let burn down to the filter. "Sorry for slapping you, but don't disrespect me. You understand?" Her face is lit up, all garish and unreal. I think to myself—and then I feel like an ass—she looks like such a rag, how come the priest wanted to do her?

"Yeah," I croak. My eyes smart and wince from the impact. The news won't settle, my mind can't swallow it.

Nothing seems important right now, though, except finding Spanky a pad. Not even this.

"Now are you going to ask me your question or are you going to get the hell out of my kitchen and find yourself a job."

"Uhm. Yeah. I guess so. It's my friend Spanky," I begin. But I know it's completely useless now. I start to shake my head. "It doesn't matter now, I guess."

"Just friggin' ask, Mary Margaret. I hate it when you do that."

"He's got no place to go," I say. "Derek's mom doesn't want him there anymore. He's a good kid, Mom. It would only for a little while, a few days even, til I can find him some-place else—" and I notice her face is set like stone. I don't even get to break into the whole 'we'll both get jobs' routine. She's just shaking and shaking and shaking her head.

"Weren't you listening? We don't have an income, girl. We're gonna have to start packing our bags again. And I ain't in the right mood to look after other people's children right now. They aren't stray cats, you know." She takes another big gulp of her drink, takes a minute to come up with something else. "I already got Zach to worry about, don't I? Haven't I played the good Samaritan long enough?" She stands up on her hobbled, overworked feet, disgusted, and swaggers out of the room holding her drink in front of her.

I'm so fucked up by the time I actually leave my house that I don't even know where I'm going. I let my feet just take me, like they're on some invisible path. So when I slip into the bar I'm sort of shocked at what's it's come to.

It's the first time I've seen Zach since he kissed me. I corner him away from my brothers at the pool hall where they're busy fleecing some sneering fat-walleted college kids.

I can't help but snort when I see this, thinking to myself, as long as my brothers stay good con men we won't have a problem with money. But how to break that to my mother? They're drunk, too. I can see this from the way they walk, a sort of cockragged strut around the table where they lace their cues through fingertips and move them smoothly into the pockets. Balls bouncing in the holes and the shitfaced grin on their faces saying, "Hey man, just a lucky shot." I suppose they get drunk to make the players feel better about losing all their money. But the poor guys don't know that my brothers, expert hustlers, play even better when they're tanked.

I don't like the way the day is turning out. Dust and smoke swirl in the few patches of light. Old men, beers in hand, stare at me as though I'm the second coming, and I don't look but go directly up to Zach and tap him on the shoulder, make him move away from the game.

He seems surprised that I've tracked him down here. "Bennett," I say after an uncomfortable minute where he just stares at me, an unlit smoke dangling from his lips.

"Got a light, Magpie? My fucking lighter doesn't work," he says, zipping his thumb up and down on the tab.

"As if," I say as I light his cigarette, watch the first puff fly upwards like a smoke signal. I concentrate on it, this one small, wispy strand, trying to keep myself together. "Bennett," I say. "I'm on a mission. I need your help. Well, actually, a favour to ask. For a mutual friend."

His sudden look of concern upsets me. I had my spiel all worked out until this throws me off balance. I signal to the bartender, who ignores me. "You in trouble, Magpie? You okay?"

"Fine, fine. It's not me, okay? How's your old man these days?"

"Why do you ask?"

"Because I'm asking."

"Same ole' same ole'," he says. He gives me this look, asks, "What's the deal?"

"Spanky."

"Oh-kay. I'll bite. What about Spanky."

"Well," I toss my head and feel blue clumps of hair rise and settle, "He's been out lately. Deke's mom decided her couch was better left to paying company or some such shit. Know what I mean?"

"Oh, shit, Mags."

I give Zach a hopeful look. "He'd never even know."

"Fuck, you know he lost his job again. And poor fucking Spanky. He's probably safer in the street than at my place. The old guy'd fucking notice. I'm sorry, I really wish I could do something."

A knot threatens to close off my windpipe. I bow my head so Zach can't see my face but it makes the knot in my throat worse. "You sure?"

"Mags," and he tries to take my hand, "I would do it for you—and Spanky—if I could. I know how much you like him."

"Yeah," I say, "no sweat." I can't move for a second, thinking of all the things that seem impossible.

"Ask Nat," Benny tells me. He's wearing this really kind of sick look on his face. His eyes are all scrunched up, like he can see deep into my motives. We've been talking at the door of the Underground for what seems to be forever, going back and forth as I try to explain the situation. But Benny's playing the Hood tonight, sitting on the stool reserved for bouncers, one leg hitched up on the wall. His fishing hat's pulled over one eye and he's smoking a doob in public. And I'm thinking, boy does he ever think he's hot shit tonight. I can't help wondering what happened to Benny, why he's gone so haywire lately. Of course, I think, all roads lead back to Vern the Giant Junkie.

"I did ask Nat. In fact, not only did I ask Nat, I've been to her place. There isn't enough room to swing her fucking ferrets," I say.

"Ask PK then."

"PK's not fucking here!" I scream. "What, are you a lunatic suddenly? You think I can communicate with the dead? Where the hell have you been, Benny?"

"Well there's an empty apartment then, isn't there."

"Look, I've just been talking to about every single person I know. No one seems to have any room but you, Benny." Benny ignores me for this dude who gives him a handshake, and they're all 'hey man, what's up' style for a few minutes before he turns back to me.

"Where the hell is Jackson?" I ask. But Benny just stands there and shrugs. He's not going to tell me because he doesn't want anyone to interfere.

"Whatsamatter, Benny? Where's Jackson?"

And this is where it gets incredible. He just waves me off, says, "Get lost, Magpie. We're so done here."

And then I know. Benny's gone over and I doubt he'll be back. He thinks he's *bigger* than the club now. He's probably got himself all taken care of with the Hell's Angels or some shit, and now he just wants to be an asshole. Fuck all the people who *used* to be his friends. I want to punch him in the mouth. I want to knee his balls and watch blood rise out of his mouth. I don't know if I'm so pissed at him because he brought up PK's disappearance, or if it's mostly because Benny's such a dimwitted tightwadded asshole. I mean, with an attitude like his, the Angels are going to bury him in a matter of months. And I can't stop myself. I do the stupidest thing imaginable. I snap.

"Listen, fuckhead," I finally find my words, poking my stupid-ass finger into his chest. "You're the one who brought him in here like this. Besides, you got the space, Benny. Don't be such an asshole. You can do this. You owe him to get him out of this. You understand me?"

"I don't owe no one shit. You understand *me*?" His eyes are shooting black pistols. He stands so close to me that I know he's passed that line. That crazy, imaginary line. And I also know that right now my brothers' reputations won't count for shit if he feels like pulling something.

"Fuck you," I spit off to the side, moving out of range.

"Maybe later, bitch," Benny says and turns his back to me. I can feel his coldness stretching out across the whole god-damn city.

I'm still snarling over Benny the next morning when it hits me that maybe the asshole was on to something. I mean, PK may be gone, but maybe his apartment isn't. Before I meet up with Spanky I figure I ought to know one way or the other.

But when I get there I put my hand on PK's door and wish like hell that he was around to help. I pace the building six times before I get myself under control. And it's so weird, when I walk in. Nothing's changed inside. It still smells like flowers and rotting fruit and incense. The same wooden counter with the ancient cash register. And Mr. Sing, hurling some Cantonese at his wife, who's busy uncrating wilted lettuce in the back.

Looking at Mr. Sing I almost loose my nerve. I mean, I'm so out of options. I've phoned everyone I have a number for, have personally gone to plead Spanky's case with Derek and his mom. I even went around asking the staff at the Underground for help. But then I keep seeing the look on

Spanky's face when I told him I'd find him a place. So I smooth my messy hair, fix the waist of my skirt, plaster a smile on my face and dive in.

After about thirty seconds Mr. Sing goes, "No no no, girl." This is his way of being friendly. I'm sure of it. "Your friend left here, didn't come to work no more. Just left. No more of you two. That's it." He waves his hands at me like he's shooing off a small dog.

"But—listen, Mr. Sing, this guy is a real stand-up guy—"

"Sorry. No. My wife, she don't have it no more." He grumbles over the cash register and turns his head back to the produce bill beside him. Another round of Cantonese is thrown at the woman who always looks bagged. "You go now," he says. "No more of you young guys. You *punks*."

And now I'm feeling on a bit more familiar territory. It's like everything lately—it sucks. I mean, I don't really blame Mr. Sing. He just wants his money. But here I've been taught to think that there are all these people on our side, and there's still no place for Spanky to go. It's like the club's been going through some personality crisis lately.

As if on cue it begins to rain outside, first one drop and then a torrent. The sky comes down in hunks of polluted rain. Stepping out of the shelter of the store eaves I'm wondering what the hell is happening. It's almost like there's this huge conspiracy to prevent things from getting any better. Or maybe it was always like this. I'm too young to remember.

"Spanky? Hey, hon, you okay?"

"Yeah," he scratches, "Just a little tired today. Didn't sleep well last night." I'm under a store stoop with him, watching him shiver away, and feeling kind of like a zombie myself. I'm practically numb inside, shivering with rain and cold.

And worse is Spanky. I can practically see him tossing on

the park bench, his toes clenched up inside the shoes with the gaping holes in them, soaking in the rain. Draped over with his army jacket, pulled close in case some one wants to take it off him. And the cold feeling that sweeps inside a person, drawn up tight inside, without any place else to put it.

"Spanks, listen. I've talked to just about everybody I know."

Laughing a little, he says, "Hey, no room at the inn, right?"

"Yah, that's about it. My mom just lost her job and Zach's dad—"

"You don't have to explain. It's okay. Really." He sits up taller, leaning up against the closed-up store.

"I'm just saying I need a little more time. Ask some more people at the club, y'know? We've just started here," I tell him. I'm not ready to tell him the truth yet, that I'm at the end of a very short rope. So I have to ask what no one wants to ask some one who's on the streets. Trying to sound normal I go, "Hey. Uhm. Do you—uhm—do you have anyone you can call, Spanky? I mean—"

"Doesn't matter, y'know. I'll be alright. You didn't have to go through so much trouble for me."

"I don't think so man. It's gonna be fall soon. You gotta have a place to go."

"I can go to the shelters and soup kitchens like everyone else."

"Come on, Spanky. That's some horrible shit."

"Fuck," he says, poofing it out like a small explosion. Every time this kid swears I'm surprised. "They've just gotta make things as hard as possible, don't they?"

"Spanky, listen. We'll go back to my place right now, kay? I'll make us some KD and coffee and we'll sit around and listen to my mom's crappy ABBA records. And then maybe you can call your folks and they can send you some cash. Okay?" I offer it to him before I let myself remember what it's like at home. But then again, there's always the chance that if Fran sees him she'll take him under her wing. Unless she's crying. Or drunk. Or both.

He just sits there for a moment, eyes squeezed shut so tight that the veins move in and out. Absently he rubs the spot where his mouse used to sit, just inside his armpit, and he gives me this stoic, shutter-eyed nod.

But when we get to my place Fran's out for the day. I don't know whether to think of it as a miracle or a curse. The record is blasting 'Does your mother know that you're out' when I've got Spanky close enough to the phone that he might just pick it up.

"But it's long distance," he says. He looks scared. He kind of looks like a street where all the power's gone out.

"Chill," I say, trying to sound relaxed even though I know she'll definitely freak, "I'll shoot my mom a couple of bucks."

"Where are you gonna get a couple bucks," his grin comes out shyly.

"Her purse. Failing that I got brothers, don't I?"

"Yeah, guess you do, don't you." I can read his face like it's a comic book caption: '*You're so lucky.*'

But I can't deal with telling Spanky what's really going on in the old Smith household. He'd really freak out, and then he'd disappear. He's so polite I think he'd sooner die than put someone out.

I say, "You got any brothers? Sisters?"

"Naw. Got a step-brother, though. He's six."

"Cool, but not old enough to deliver you some cash."

"Yeah. Whatever," he shrugs. "I never met him. He's my mom's husband's kid. Never met him either."

"Oh. So who you gonna call?"

"My father, I guess." I hear it come out like 'My f*aa*-ther'. He turns to the phone and stares at it like it's going to bite him. It's like those surreal commercials where the kid's in the phone booth and it's raining fucking monkeys, and all you hear is, "Mom, Dad, it's me, Mikey," or some shit. Except that this scene is in my run-down, crappy livingroom, ABBA warbling in the background, and somehow I don't expect it to go well. Those are government funded ads, after all, that tell people kids are delighted to go home after a 'tiny tiff', even if their parents are complete assholes. The phone rings and rings and rings. And then finally Spanky's mouth is gaping.

He finally says, "Dad?—don't hang up—it's me. Lawrence." There's an awful, loaded pause on his end. His face scrunches up so tight that I'm worried it's going to snap right off. I hear, "No. No, I'm not a drug addict—" as I'm backing out of the room. I practically run into my room, shut the door, cover my ears with my hands. Stare at my shirt that's hanging on the wall, staring back at me. I wait a good five minutes, and by the time I come out Spanky's off the phone. He's staring at the ringer in disbelief. Like he's just seen his whole pathetic life flash in front of his eyes.

"What happened," I say, as if I can't figure it out. I suppose I'm trying to put a good face on it, smile while everything goes nuts.

He's just glaring at the phone like it's beaten the crap out of him. "He hung up on me. He fucking hung up on me. He doesn't want me to go home." I reach over, thinking of putting my arm around him, but he backs away. He looks like he's about to cry. I could choke on all the bile I feel coming up. It threatens to eat through my fillings.

"Shit, Spanky. Shit, God, fuck, I'm so sorry." I try to reach out to him again but his body whips back like it's been slapped.

"Don't—don't touch me. Okay, Magpie? I'll be okay." He's trying to shake himself back together, refuses to cry. It's something I understand well. It's something I even respect. Personally, I'm about as close to crying as I've been since I was a kid.

"Shh. Shh," I say, panicking a bit. "Can you call your mom, Spanky?"

"I don't know where—she—is—" it's like he's talking through cotton he's so choked up. "I don't know where she went. She left and I never heard from her again. Except a postcard that said she was married again. She sent me a postcard from Vegas. She and her new husband and his kid."

"Maybe your dad knows where. Maybe I could—"

"NO. No more, okay? I'm tired. I gotta go. Take care of yourself, eh Magpie?" he says. And he's getting his tattered coat on, washing his hands in the kitchen sink, splashing his face with water. "Thanks for trying. At least you tried," he tells me, and I know he's in trouble because he won't look me in the eyes. It's in the eyes where you can see the roads a person can walk on and which ones they can't. And then he's gone, just vanishes out my door like his ass is on fire, as if he'd never even been there. The only evidence of his passing through is stacked up on the counter. Dirty bowls rimmed with the congealed remains of Kraft Dinner.

We All Fall Down

I'm starting to think of life as a science experiment, where you're trying to change lead into gold, but all you do is watch everything turn to shit.

The last time I saw PK the look on his face reminded me of Jessie a million years ago. It was the expression of someone who's already gone. Someone who has it in their mind that they're doing the right thing by not looking too closely, but closer still at something else, something I can't see yet.

And then there's Spanky. When he left my apartment he had the same sort of look to him. It hooked like a shadow across his nose. It was his own peace that he carried away with him, as if he'd already solved all the world's problems and his own while he was at it. Something so sudden that I thought I heard a click. In the time span it would take to snap my fingers, his eyes opened wide and I swear—he must have stopped feeling anything. Snap snap, and he was out the door. I didn't even have time to tell him that it wasn't the end of the world. He probably wouldn't have believed me anyway.

Sometimes I try to imagine what people do, what they're like when I'm not with them. Like Nat after a long night of slinging drinks, when she goes home to her pet ferrets. Or Fran when she's off cleaning the church, or cozying up to her boyfriend the priest. I've tried to figure out what's it's like to be Zach when his old cubist comes home and beats on him. Or my brothers—what are they thinking when they're off playing the small-time hoods?

It's always an illusion when I see someone and I say, "See you tomorrow." Because everything is balanced on the fact that there will be a tomorrow with this person in it. Anything could happen. People leave. People go away and you never hear what really happened to them—you can only make it up, try to step inside someone and figure out why it all sucks so much.

What I think happened, when Spanky left me, was this:

He started walking. He walks like an old man, bent and tired, especially right at the small of his back where he feels the oldest. Shuffling his feet he finds himself going through the park that looks sort of tired too. It's a gray, overcast day. Everything is wilting and falling down. The air smells like rain, iron-tinged and wet. There are all these women there with kids. Maybe they're the babysitters, nannies, teenage mothers—I don't know. But the kids are all screaming and shrieking. I imagine he puts his hands to his ears, really slowly. I imagine he wants to stop those ears up. It's too loud, too raw. It's a reminder of all the stuff he can't be anymore.

He's been walking all night. It feels like weeks.

The rubber and canvas of his shoes are so dissolved now that it's almost impossible to keep moving. His toes stretch and rub at the exposed edges, keeping him constantly there in the present, there in each step that sort of jolts through him like an electric shock. When he lands on a rock he's got to pause and wait for the pain to ebb away before he goes again. He keeps walking though, right through the park. Maybe the colours of the leaves remind him of a leaf collection he had as a kid, I don't know, but he goes through the park and stops there, on the concrete sidewalks, before he moves again. I see him wrapping his fingers up inside those fraying sleeves, tightening the fabric around his fingers that are only sort of clean. A shiver goes through him, even though it's the kind of warm summer day that makes you think of words like lazy.

All over the park the grass is tall, pocked with the white billows of dandelion fluff. The kind of seeds with brown roots and white crowns, the kind you blow on in order to have a wish come true. I'm thinking he probably didn't know what to wish for any more. I imagine his confusion in seeing such an abundance of them—literally a carpet of them. The grass looks like an ocean, like a sea of never-come-true wishes. If he cocks his head to one side, the grass sounds like tongues lapping a bowl of water. He thinks of cars on a rain-soaked street that look so bright on the pavement, so clear and colourful through the puddled asphalt he thinks it may be possible to step into another world.

It's fucking madness and he knows it. He knows his mind is fuzzy from lack of sleep, from the unexpected arrival of food into his system, and something else. Something that pushes at his guts but he can only feel it like the dull edge of a headache, something he's got to prevent from blossoming. He looks back at the park. The scene is blurry.

He thinks everything is water. He thinks he can crawl into it, float on it. He thinks that he can wash the dirt from his body and be clean again. This is how tired he is. His mind plays tricks on him. I think in his mind he was swimming. His feet glide-shuffle along the concrete. He walks through the traffic as though the cars are silvery fish that want to nibble on his fingers as they pass. Trees waving to him in the wind.

This is where things get hazy for me. Did he walk through the subway entrance by accident, or did he think it was the perfect place for him? Could he hear the roar of the trains before he stepped down, before he jumped the turnstiles and strolled along, down into the bowels of the city?

The busker in the corners beside the stairs evidently didn't stop him—not the guy playing the Neil Young tunes with the long dirty dreads and Birkenstocked feet. Not the guy in the gray suit hocking his *Watchtower* magazines. Everything must have sounded distorted, like it would if you lived in a fish bowl. Everything must have sounded strange except the roar of the train.

I'm sure he picked the track at random. I mean, I don't think he even had a coin to toss. They split and you have to choose. When he arrived at the bottom level there was a train pulling out on the opposite side. The metallic empty sound of the chimes as the door closed. Faces pressed outward, mouths puckered bows against the glass. And the train disappeared down the dark tunnel, a metallic eel skidding along the tracks with a wake of blue and yellow sparks.

He walked to the farthest end of the platform. This was a conscious decision. Standing on a bright yellow line speckled with dark dots of gum and ash, the raised bumps of the rubber border the colour and texture of exotic fish, he was poised for the exact moment the train would enter the station.

What I imagine is this: maybe he was coming to his senses at that moment. Maybe he was starting to think things over, to panic at the leap he'd have to take. Maybe he was so miserable he started to cry a little. Nobody came to help. Nobody asked him if he was okay. Nobody told him everything was alright, they'd help. Not a single person pulled the goddamn subway alarm. And so when he heard the train coming closer, its approach to the station good and fast—and it sounded like the coming of a tidal wave, it sounded like something that could make him feel better—he shushed all those voices inside him.

His shoes had given out, see. He couldn't walk one more frigging step without new shoes. And anyway, he was too damned tired to tie his shoelaces. So he opted for peace and quiet beneath the waves. He opted for sleep. And he waited for it to creep closer, closer, so close he could step inside it and ride the wave home. And then he did.

The End of the World

It began with Jessie, just before the end of the world. The day before her thirteenth birthday the three of us went roaming. PK's dad had gone haywire again over who the fuck knows what, so we were keeping Peek occupied and out of the way. A plane shredded the sky with its supersonic drone as we went through the streets with their tiny, bent brick houses and rusting porches. PK kicked some glass off the sidewalk and onto the street. "Kids walk on these sidewalks," he complained. "Little kids who don't know enough to wear their damn shoes." Jessie and I giggled, called him, as we sometimes did, 'Saint Peckoria'. We turned onto the main drag. People were sitting outside at the cafes, sipping their lattes and smoking. PK took the cue and produced a couple of cigarettes.

"So what are we going to do for your birthday," I asked Jessie.

"Dunno," she shrugged. "It's always a bad time of year. Everyone on vacation and stuff."

"Really. What are we, chopped liver? Do you see us goin' on vacation?"

"I was thinking about having you guys over for dinner."

PK winked at me, saying, "Hmm. A home-cooked meal at the Belson residence? Sounds like it's my birthday."

"Then I thought maybe my parents could give us enough money to go to the movies."

It was summertime. In another week or so school was going to start. People walked by in their summer dresses and sandals, their shorts and t-shirts and bathing suit tops drenched in humidity. "What movie d'y'wanna see?" I said and fiddled with my cigarette. Pete had been teaching me how to hold them right, behind Joe's back, like the old guys do in the black and white movies. Fingers tough and relaxed. So we duck into this bookstore to check out the papers long enough to figure out that my all-time favourite movie, *Night of the Comet,* was playing on Jessie's birthday—and got kicked out about 5 seconds later. Apparently they didn't appreciate kids who could read. We were just strolling along, minding our own business, when we hit this commotion. All these people were standing around gawking and spitting where the subway grates blow out the warm air from below. But they split their ranks pretty easy. You could tell there was something uncool up ahead.

I heard him before I could see him. His raspy baritone all warped with drink. "You bastards don't know—goddamn thing," he screamed. The big joke in our neighbourhood at the time was that if you threw a stray cat you'd hit a stray person, so I'd only thought, okay, another raving looney tune.

This crowd of people stood around as though they were watching a peep show. I got this terrible creeping feeling in my gut, and then I saw it. Through some legs at first, then between shoulders. A filthy ragman with his white chunky hair all plastered up. I'd seen him before, knew who he was. His green Sally Ann pants that he normally wore rode low, down to his pubic hair. The wire he usually wrapped around the waist had somehow come loose. Oh yeah, I recognized him. He was the guy who usually had tiny pastel rubber bands tying his beard and hair into tiny spikes. At the moment he was using blackened fingers to prop himself off the cardboard he was sitting on. Through the grime tracks his face was blushing crimson. Bulbous broken veins in his nose were shining like a radar screen. Red splotches on his forehead, his shirtless chest. Sweating. "It's the *end,* stupid goddamns. The end. It'll teach you never to—" He raised one hand as though deflecting a blow. "You're all *finished,* you evil demon spawn hated of God," he roared, "the *end of you all.*" As if my hair wasn't standing up enough by then.

It took a minute to sink in. I looked around for Jessie, to

make sure she wasn't getting knocked around by the crowd. And I guess that's why the scene finally pieced all together for me. The people—standing, watching. This man, his pants almost off, almost naked, a half empty bottle of yellow after-shave beside him. A ferocious odour peeling off him, sweet fake flower smell and baby vomit. Other people walking by, looking down and then away. And then the worst part of it.

There were these kids, maybe a bit older than us, with these hockey sticks and a puck. And they're shooting at this raving man, knocking at him with their pucks and curved wood blades, "He shoots, he *scores!*" People just standing around, playing the spectators.

I could feel my face hit the boiling point. I knew PK was there because I suddenly felt the pressure of his hand on my shoulder, trying to keep me back. I turned back and looked at him, at his mouth dropped into a perfectly round 'oh,' and for a second all I could do was *stare*.

"What the hell is wrong with you people? What the hell're you doing?" I suddenly screamed, and I could hardly believe it had been said, out there in the open. I roared through the crowd, hurling insults until I got close to one of the kids who was playing target practice with the guy. He was laughing. It struck me then—this kid thinks it's funny.

Before I knew it I'd pushed this guy who was much bigger than me almost to the ground. He caught himself with his hands, and I was about to start pummelling him. Of course, he was so dumb it took him a second to realize that he was the one being pushed around now, and by a girl no less. But when he did clue in I started to rethink the whole thing. He gave me the kind of look that told me what he was going to do next.

He was going to take me down. His hockey stick went up. He was about to bring it down on my head and all of these stupid dingbats, I thought, were going to stand around and clap. To this day I don't know what made me think of it. A total MacGyver move—I slipped down to the cement and rolled over. I heard the crack of wood on cement where he'd missed me, and got up and ran. Steps beside me, behind me, like I was leaving an echo chamber trail. Jess and PK were trying to keep up, and beyond them, in the distance, four big kids were dropping their hockey gear and coming after us like the hounds of fucking hell.

So two days later, on Jess's birthday, we stuck close to home. We were pretty quiet, not wanting to say much about it. I mean, it felt like this gigantic omen telling us to watch our asses, but what were we supposed to do except stay out of the way? So we played double dutch. Rectangle. We even played with her dumb barbies—the ones I'd pierced about a year before—because she wanted to.

PK hadn't arrived yet. He was really late. I didn't know if those kids got a good look at him or not, and the night before, when I'd called, no one answered the phone. Underneath the sun and fun there was this massive knot of panic. Jessie and me just kept at it, trying to pretend it wasn't bugging the shit out of us.

It got to be dinner time and Peek still hadn't shown. Jessie's mom had gone homemade Italian with garlic bread. We drank these exotic Shirley Temples with dinner and her parents sipped red wine. We were going to have nanaimo bars and ice cream and cake for dessert. Like always, the TV was on while we ate. I remember I kept thinking, everything would be so beautiful if PK were there. The light was soft and warm outside, and like always Jessie's dad had his eyes trained at the TV set in the livingroom. I was busy stuffing food into my mouth as if it was the last meal I'd ever eat.

So the phone rang right as we were eating dinner. Her

mother walked up to the counter where the phone was. She picked it up and said: "Hello? Yep—yep, hang on, she's right here." Jessie's beautiful young mom handed me the phone. She mouthed at me, hand over the receiver, "I think it's important." I started quaking, knowing that any news was bad news, but I took the phone anyway.

"Hello?" I saw Jessie, her fork still poised in hand, walk into the livingroom. She sank down in front of the TV set but I couldn't see what was so interesting.

"Hello?" There was someone gulping on the other line, as if the person was trying not to make any noise. Trying, I thought, not to cry. "Who's there?"

Jessie's mom swivelled her head in my direction. "PK," she mouthed at me, her hand curling around her lips like an imaginary bugle.

"Peek? 'S 'at you?"

"Mags."

"God, PK, what happened? Are you okay? Is everyone okay at my house? Where're you calling from?"

"'M'at a pay phone." He took a deep breath before saying anything else. "In the hood."

"What happened, Peek? You better tell me right now."

"It ain't your mom or anything. I need—uh." He started crying. I'd never heard PK cry before, not even after taking a beating.

"Peek!" I yelled. But still nothing came.

And then: "They threw me out. They fucking threw me out. But first he fucking—God I fucking hate them."

"Holy sh—hockey. Are you okay? They can't do that, can they? I mean, you ain't done nothing. You're only thirteen, for Chri—I mean, for crying out loud." He was sobbing now, all-out bawling in a pay phone, somewhere where the tough guys could see him and jump him for being a crybaby fag if they wanted to. "Peek? PK? Hell, you'll be okay." I heard him sniffling in the background, pulling himself together.

"What am I gonna do, Mags?"

"You're gonna meet me at the park in—like—fifteen minutes, okay? Fran will let you crash. It's cool, okay? She likes you. Says you're smart. Don't know where she got that big idea." He let go a burst of laughter that sounded like it had a lot of snot in it. "Okay Peek? Okay? Meet me."

"Yeah. Yeah. I'll meet you."

"We'll be okay. We'll think of something. Okay? You'll see. You'll be better than okay."

"Yeah." He said it so softly I was scared.

"So.... I'll see you soon?"

"Uh-huh. 'Kay, bye." He hung up and I imagined his eyes screwing up behind his glasses. It really pissed me off, thinking about that.

I turned around, expecting to see everyone staring at me, but everyone had gotten up and left. They were in the living-room, I supposed, so I trailed in after them. For a second I'd forgotten it was Jessie's birthday. I guessed we'd skipped the end of dinner in favour of opening presents. Her parents were in their usual position on the little brown Sears couch. Jessie was sitting there, on her hands and knees. Her fork was sticking up, still covered in tomato sauce and cheese.

So I was looking around, trying to figure out what was going on. Nobody was opening presents or anything. The Belsons were watching the news. And I was thinking, how festive, when I looked over at the screen.

There'd been a plane crash. I didn't know where. It was a charred, smoking hush of a plane cradled in trees. There was nothing left. They suddenly cut to this picture of a little girl walking beside the Kremlin. She smiled for the cameras. Waving. Collecting a bouquet of flowers from this old

Russian woman dressed all in black, waving a white hand-kerchief at her. Flashbulbs going off like tiny bombs. It was her. Samantha, of the same last name. The Samantha who was going to make the world a better, safer place to live. I don't know—this giant shiver came over me, this quick exhaustion, when I realized what had happened.

My legs went gooey. I don't know who I asked—maybe just the quiet, quiet room. I said, "Is she dead? Did she die?" No one answered. I don't think they heard me.

And it almost seemed like an accident, because the very next second I got my answer. This reporter was on the scene, a woman with her flipped-up Farrah 'do' and bright blue eye shadow. The plane's corpse, cordoned off with bright police tape, smouldered behind her. "As you can see behind me," she said all deadpan. "The plane was destroyed. There were no survivors. Officials think that all eight passengers on board, including Samantha Smith and her father, Arthur Smith, died instantly."

For just one second I had this crazy feeling. I was taken up by this gleam of silver and everything was in slo-mo. Caught in this terrible vertigo. Like I was in free fall, and everything was plunging into blackness. I was in the plane. I was on that plane with her, beside her. The cabin shook, its bolts coming undone. The windows rattled. Everything was flying around, up and down. Cups, saucers, little paper barf bags with streams of barf cartwheeling through the air. Magazines and newspapers, blankets and sandals. But we sat there, holding hands. Me and Samantha. As if we were the best of friends, as if we really were cousins. She stared at me, looking kind of relaxed, like she knew this is how it would turn out from day one.

And I don't know. In this little hallucination I was staring back at her. And I felt how sad the both of us were, deep down, under the fear and all that. The engine was roaring, people had stopped screaming and started praying. It felt like all the air was being ripped out of our lungs, it was getting smoky in the cabin. I squeezed her hand tighter.

The plane slammed into the trees, breaking into the dark limbs and scattering branches that caught on fire the moment they were touched. I wanted to scream, but just then everything jarred, like the plane was actually doing a loop on a roller coaster track. Samantha's hand flew out of mine and a second later we hit the ground. There was this momentous burst of light. All around everything was shattering, turning to glass and dust, and the explosion was like a nuclear blast licking up everything in its path.

Until that second, when I snapped out of it, I had no idea that this kid had meant so much to me. "She's really dead?" I asked again. It wouldn't stick. I tried to hold the reality in my head but it kept disappearing. But my nostrils still smelt burning trees. It was like I'd been on a cigarette bender and could even feel the path of smoke trickling between my mouth and nose. "She's *dead*? She can't be dead."

And then I remembered Jessie. I remembered not just that it was her birthday, not even that Samantha Smith had actually accomplished all the stuff that Jessie wanted to do. What I thought about was the way Jessie had looked at me, tears climbing down her cheeks, when we first heard about Samantha. I remembered Jessie in her closet, wanting me to climb in as though that could save us both, because there was room for two, and the teeth, loose and floating, that had attacked her in her dream. And I thought of PK, and the bombs.

I forced my eyes away from the black hole on TV, over to her. Jessie had sunk down into a ball on the carpet. Her mom was going, "Jessie? Jessica. Sweetie, get up. Jessie?" Jess was insensible. Totally out of it. All the light and colour had drained out of her face. And suddenly I just *knew*. Jessie was right there with me, with the little girl. She was stuck on that falling plane too. Stuck in her worst nightmare. Right then I thought about what some kids had told me: that if you had a falling dream and you hit the ground you never wake up. You die. That's what I thought was happening to Jessie.

I stood there for a moment, not knowing what to do. I thought about telling the Belsons that I had to go, mentioning politely that PK had an emergency and I had to help him. I thought about trying to help Jessie—explaining things to Jessie's parents. I thought about telling them that Jessie slept in her closet every night, and about Samantha, and about what it all meant.

By then Jessie's mom was leaning over her, giving Jessie's face these little butterfly slaps. She started screaming, "Jessica! Jessie Belson, stop it right now!" Her mom was just freaking. But Jessie looked exactly like she did when she was awake-asleep in the closet. Unseeing eyes, her body curled up and protecting itself, like a snail in its shell. Like she could build herself a bomb shelter and stay there for a million years.

I caught a glimpse of Samantha's mom on TV as I was backing carefully out of the room. She looked so fucking sad. It felt like all the breath was being knocked right out of me. Then the screen flashed someone else. A portly guy, his big bald spot shining under the sun. He said that Mrs. Smith had written this. A message for the press. There were dozens of microphones pointed at the guy, and I made my bare feet quiet on the floor so I could hear as I went for the door.

"Each generation," he read, slowly and carefully. He paused every word or two as though the wind had been socked out of him, too. "—contributes a building block for the next generation. As individuals, we are the particles of earth from which the blocks are formed—I hope Samantha—

and Arthur—have helped us realize—how important each of us can be."

The door didn't even make a click. I hadn't said goodbye. And the next time I'd seen Jessie she'd been on the bus, her eyes looking through me, X-rays of a future gone awry.

Waking the Dead

The second I left Jessie's that awful night it felt like something was pulling at my neck hairs. Like nothing would ever be the same again. It wasn't quite dark, but the moon was already glowing like a cat's-eye marble, and the first stars were beginning to make the scene. It was kind of like a kick to the teeth, seeing that pearly sky. Where the hell was the fire? Where was the torn corner, the smoke trail to mark where Samantha Smith had fallen through? My feet thudded on the sidewalk but I kept my eye on the sky, wondering if the nukes would tumble down after her.

My sweet, gentle PK had just been through the ride of his life. He reeked of beer. Most of his hair was plastered down with it where his dad had lobbed bottles at his head. There were cuts on his face and hands, tiny scratches and bubbles of blood that had risen and dried. He had a black eye. Looking at PK I finally understood what my brothers had been telling me—to rely only on them, on the network of friends and allies that they'd built up, an arsenal for my own use.

I felt like pulling a Jessie, but I didn't have the luxury of collapsing on the floor. PK needed me. We were all alone, but I figured we'd burn holding hands if we had to. So I took PK home. I bathed his wounds. My mother tisk-tisked, shook her head, let out some Gaelic epithets. She rubbed disinfectant over his eye, on his burns. We put him on the couch and wrapped him in the extra blanket. I fed him tea and toast, soup and coffee. I watched him pace and try to figure out how it had all gone so wrong.

And all the while it felt like I was starring in a horror movie. But the horror was actually this world that was ending, always over. This world where little girls who only wanted to grow up without being incinerated, fell out of the sky and were reduced to ashes. This place where people who I thought were pretty rich, pretty happy, couldn't get off the floor, people bowled over by this one little girl's death. This was the place where the smartest kid I knew had to fight just to get through the afternoon.

It wasn't just Samantha Smith that Jessie mourned. It was the death of her faith. Just like me. Like the flip of a switch, the press of a button—it was gone. How could any one have faith in a world like this? How could people believe in world leaders, in governments, in good intentions? Or parents, or safe places, or even that a kid could grow up and make the world a different kind of place? I've been thinking that maybe a part of me has always been like Jessie—trapped on the same damned burning plane. I never quite climbed out of the wreckage, or at least not in one piece.

So the minute Spanky left my place it was like I'd thrown this invisible pair of hands into the air and screamed *I give up*. I don't know what I was thinking—but I don't know that I thought he'd go and get himself killed. I should have gone after him, gone looking for him, but I didn't. It was like the hopelessness of it all sucked me up and spit me out. So instead I just sat there for a long time, listening to the quiet. It was like I was the last person in the world.

When my brothers got home I hid in my bedroom, spun around for a few seconds, tried to sort myself out. The first thing I spotted was my new t-shirt staring at me from the wall. I unpinned it and slipped it on. It smelled like the streets—clouds of car smoke and cigarettes and grass. Hot dogs and sun. And I guess it all made me pretty tired, because I just sank like a stone into sleep.

By the time I woke up it was the next day and the apartment was empty. I didn't know where anyone was. I paced, drank coffee, kept my hands busy, smoked too much. I spent an hour at a time shooting the phone dirty looks. Eventually

I called around, to see if anyone had run into Spanky. I even broke down and called Benny, and even he started to sound concerned. Maybe it was because I was hysterical, talking a mile a minute.

It had to have been around eight by the time my mom wandered in the door, looking like a bag of somebody's left-overs. The kitchen had been made spotless, the livingroom—hell, I'd even cleaned the bathroom. Fran blinked a few times, looked around, took a good long look at me. She dropped her big, leather old lady's purse on the floor. She said, "What's wrong, Mary Margaret." And I cracked. I burst into big fucking nervous crybaby tears.

But by the time I'd gotten myself into a state where I could answer Fran with anything resembling a coherent sentence my brothers walked in the door. They were laughing, talking, all happy and jokey. Pete had a liquor store bag in his hand. Joe had a case of beer. "Hey Mags," Joe said, "we're doing tequila poker tonight—you in?" After a second or two they'd chilled a bit and realized that Fran was sitting there rubbing my back, brushing blue bangs out of my red red eyes.

"Joseph, Peter," my mother said. She had one of her iron hooks in her voice. "Make yourselves scarce for a minute." Poof—they disappeared.

"Mary Margaret," she turned back to me, all soft and coaxing, "what in God's name is going on with you?"

"Ah, Mom," I said, and didn't know where to begin.

The thing is, people who talk about the end of the world always have a date. They say stuff like, "We're sure it will end on September 4th this year—or next." Or: "January 1st, 2000—we've made all the calculations. We're absolutely convinced." I'm not going to lie and say I'm any different. In my brief experience this is the day that always gets me, the day I walk on eggshells. Jessie's birthday. I'd been waiting for the day it caught up with me, tripped me up. Eventually, I knew, it would come back to deal me a hand. In the end, I figure, there are no such things as survivors.

Just then the buzzer rang. Out of the corner of my eye I caught Joe slinking towards it. Fran snapped, "Joseph Smith, who the hell is that?"

"Uhm," he said. "It's just some of the gang, Mom. It's tequila poker night. I can tell them to go away if you want."

Fran looked over at me. But I blinked, said, "It's okay. Really. I don't care." Fran nodded at Joe, and he buzzed in. Maybe I did care. Maybe I wanted witnesses—I don't know. It's like I just *knew* that things were about to become seriously fucked.

A few seconds later Nat and Derek sauntered in wearing sombreros and carrying a Texas mickey of tequila. A few minutes after that Zack knocked on the door and let himself in. And I have to admit, I was relieved. All attention turned towards mixing drinks and spreading peanuts around the kitchen table.

"Mags," Joe came up to me. I was still a fixture on the couch. "You want me to pour you a drink?"

"Yeah," I said. "Make it a double."

"Hey kid, you okay?"

"Sure," I said. I think I tried to laugh. "No sweat. Perfect."

"You wanna play? Can we deal you in?" I went all fidgety. Joe gave me his concerned older brother look.

"Naw," I said. "Maybe later. I think I'll just sit here and watch."

Then he saw my shirt. "That new? It's really cool," he said.

Everything felt like it was running on borrowed time. I could feel it—hear it—the ticking sound winding down. Fran disappeared into her room. The gang was swinging into their second round, cards and grumbling passed across the table. I started to relax a bit, even smiling now and again as Nat trounced the boys. The buzzer went off again, sounding like an egg timer. Derek stuck his head up out of his cards, asked, "Is that Benny?"

Pete shrugged, shook his head. I slipped off the couch and over to the intercom, buzzed in. I got all hopped up, thinking, maybe PK's come home. Maybe it's Spanky. Maybe everything's okay. A few seconds later a heavy knock sounded on the door. I opened up. My eyes came level to a couple of dark chests, the kind with badges.

"Ahem," the first one coughed. "We're looking for someone named 'Magpie'?" And then I knew.

Spanky had stashed my phone number and name in the top pocket of his army jacket. The police didn't know squat about this poor-ass kid whose body they'd scraped from the front of a train, so they came looking for me. Fran sat beside me, holding my hand as they fired off question after question, sometimes stopping to ask someone else. Joe and Pete fixed everyone triples at that point, all except me, since the police were there and I'm underage. They filled out forms, made me write down what I knew. The freaky thing was, I probably knew Spanky the best out of everyone, and even I didn't know dick. I had no idea who or where his parents were, who had abandoned him, except they were from up north and Spanky's first name—his real name—was Lawrence. I told them, in front of Fran, about the phone call, that his dad's number would turn up on our phone bill. Fran said, "Good girl." The cops said it was a "lucky break."

When Fran finally let them out, over an hour later, everyone was still there. Except for the chain-smoking it was like we were playing some huge round of frozen tag. Staring at the table, at their hands. At me. Like I was some sort of freak show attraction.

Finally Derek broke it up, saying, "Mags, I'm so fucking sorry. I mean, we didn't know it was that bad."

"I really don't want to hear it," I kind of mumbled. I needed a fucking drink.

"I really liked that kid."

"Shut UP! Shut up, just shut up," My hands clamped over my ears and I stamped my feet like a four-year-old. I couldn't help it. What the fuck did they think I'd been doing?

"Hey, chill, Mags." This was Nat. Sticking up for Derek, for all of them. I saw Joe and the Twins shoot her a warning look but evidently she didn't get it. "No one could have known what was going to happen." And my head—and my mouth—went into overdrive.

The day I'd had to put my broken-up PK on my couch and watch him cry himself to sleep was the same day I thought I was witnessing the ashes of the whole goddamned world. So I put my faith in the club. Everyone needs to believe in something, right? I'd thought that members were crusaders—down and dirty in the name of justice. I thought that together we could at least hold up our crumbling corner of the map. But all I'd been taught to believe about us, all I'd come to rely on, turned out to be just another big rip-off. When it came right down to it, nobody really had the strength or the power to lift you up off your ass. No matter how long you go on the lam, or how often you sleep in your closet, it's going to keep falling down on you. Hiding, no matter where, isn't going to make it any better. That's probably why PK split. That's why Spanky died. That's why the world was always going to be over. But what I couldn't take was anymore lying. I couldn't bear to hear one more person try to cover it all up, thinking they could make it all go away.

"Don't you 'chill' me, Nat. You," I shouted, pointing my

finger at Nat's chest, "are a fucking traitor. You did this. You're all fucking *guilty*." And my finger started going off like a fucking gun, aiming at everyone in turn. "*I'm* guilty. But you know what? At least I did something. I tried. What the hell did you do? Where were you? Huh? *I* knew, Nat."

Derek looked over to Joe, mumbling, "Maybe we should go, eh? Give you guys some room—"

"Don't bother," I screamed. I didn't care what I said. They'd all failed. Every single goddamn one of them. "The Club. What a bunch of bullshit. You're all so full of it. You don't care about anyone or anything, do you?"

Black spots swam in front of my eyes as I ran outside into the streets. I think if it had just been about Spanky I would have been able to mouth off pretty good. But it was just like Spanky said: a house of cards. As soon as you think you've got one built up, some wind or God or *something* just knocks it all over. And there you are, flat on your ass. Covered in debris.

The park was pretty empty for a dripping hot summer night. This cool wind was picking up, sucking the dust and litter off the streets. Dark, rumbling clouds rolled in and knocked the rest of the light out of the sky. Flopping myself on the ground, I lit a cigarette and stared up at the darkness. I don't know how long I lay there in the dark, just smoking and listening to the gusting wind. It just about killed me to think that no one was there to catch Spanky's fall.

A huge crack of lightning pealed overhead, a rumble behind it. Drops started pelting down like tiny hands, slapping my bare wrists and arms, my face, my legs. My cigarette fizzled out and I was left holding this stupid unsmokeable smudgy thing. I didn't know whether to laugh or cry, it was all so stupid. I wanted to call someone, but I couldn't think of anyone.

So instead I ran over to a store stoop and just stood there, watching all these people go by. Dealers and peelers, a few parental types walking around with their strollers, old Asian ladies with their shopping bags fat with fish. And then there were all these kids like me—laughing, spitting, holding hands. It's stupid but I felt like a ghost. No one saw me standing there, and if they did they pretended they didn't.

I don't know how long I stood there, maybe an hour or so, smoking and feeling like there was a wall between me and the living, when this bum waddled up. He was one of the lifers, one of the schizo Jesus freaks of the hood who went around barefoot, swearing and cursing and praying all at the same time. So when he stopped in front of me I was waiting for him to lose it on me. But I guess he was having a good night because just looked at me and said, "Spare some change, young lady. I've got needs."

"Yeah, I hear you." I started going through my jean-short pockets but all I had was a dime, a small ball of lint, and a last cigarette. I was glad someone had finally noticed me but I couldn't figure out why it was the one guy who literally smelled like shit. Why was it the one guy who needed to take my last cigarette and my only dime?

So a few minutes later I was feeling good and sorry for myself, and the rain really started to let loose. People started running by with newspapers over their heads, their shoes making those clomping splat noises. I tried to pull out a smoke before I remembered I'd given my last one away, and suddenly I knew why people stick that last honking needle in their arm, or why someone decides it's easier to hang themselves rather than tie up their shoelaces and make coffee in the morning. It's just rain but it's cold, it has weight, and it's always coming down on you, all the time. The end of the world isn't just one thing. It's more like a chain gang that wears you down until the fireworks at the finale.

So I've been huddled in my room ever since. I hear the

phone ring about every 10 seconds, people talking in hushed voices. My brothers, my mother, even Zach, occasionally knock on the door, trying to call me out. I haven't even changed my clothes. Every now and again, when I remember, I look down at my shirt and it bores into my brain. A is for Apocalypse. V is for violence. It seems like a fucking party out there and I don't give a shit. As far as I'm concerned it's too late for their fucking sympathy.

I am so bloody tired. I'm exhausted from losing all the time, of knowing that it all gets lost over and over again. I don't want to watch the world end any more. And finally I'm able to dive into a deep sleep with no planes, no bombs, no needles, no dying. Nothing. It feels sort of like peace.

It's his phone call that wakes me up, pulls me up out of a cocoon of blankets and knees drawn up to my chest. I hear Joe outside, calling my name like I'm a lost dog. He's rattling with the lock, trying to break in. Somehow I manage to stumble to the door just as he's opening it.

"What do you want, Joe."

"You got a phone call. C'mon, hurry up. I think it's PK."

My mind is groggy. It's dark outside again. I can't remember what day it is. I don't have a clue, now, how many days PK's been missing.

"PK? *My* PK?" I say like an idiot.

Joe sort of snorts, blowing his wide nostrils that are so unlike mine. His are wide and sort of round. I suddenly can't get over how much I love Joe's nostrils. "Do you know many other shit disturbers named PK? Hurry up. Naw, leave the blanket, eh, Mags? The phone."

My feet grab the floor and I'm unsteady. Joe catches my arm, holds me up and walks me, invalid style, into the living-room. There are people sitting at the table, gaping at me. It's my mother, Pete, Zach, Nathalie, Derek—even Roddy. Aside

from the obvious list of the missing is Benny, and I'm so fucking glad he's not here. All of their eyes trained on me. It's
kind of embarrassing how concerned they all look. I glare and
then ignore them, march unsteadily over to the couch to the
phone sitting face up, right there. Two blank round ears
pointing upwards. I put my ear to it and just breathe.

There's quiet on the other end for a moment, and then I
hear it. Faint, like he's coming to me from a thousand miles
away. "Magpie?" The voice is tentative, timid. "Magpie? It's
PK."

"PK."

"Yeah, hi." I hear him let out all his air. "Hi, hi," he says.
He sounds relieved.

"Hello," I say stubbornly. I think for a moment I want to
hang up on him, but then I think the better of it. I start to cry
instead. "Peek, where are you? Why aren't you here? Where've
you been?"

"Mags, Mags, hey, shhhh. Hey, everything's going to be
okay. Right?"

But it's not going to be okay. I don't know if it will ever be
okay again. I pull the receiver away from my face and yell. "PK
you shithead! You asshole no good for nothing asswipe—"

"Mags, I'm sorry. Jesus—"

"Don't take the lord's name in vain," I yell again. He starts
giggling. He's laughing now, and somehow I think it's really
hilarious too. I can feel my chest bubbling and jerking though
no sound is coming out.

Finally he sobers up and says, "That's my Magpie."

"You are such an asshole. What happened to you?"

"I hitched a ride, went all the way out to B.C., then caught
a ride up to the Yukon. I almost made it to Alaska, except I
turned and hitched back 'cause I don't got any ID."

I just sigh. I mean—it was just so damned easy for him. To

just leave me behind, forget about me. I can't even respond. And then PK says, "Joe told me about Spanky. Mags—"

"Just shut up, PK. Just shut yer yap. And fuck you, by the way."

"Okay, I deserve that." My eyes squeeze shut. I'm trying not to cry again, not to let anything show. He says, "I'm so sorry I wasn't here. I'm so sorry, Magpie."

It's just that—just that is enough to send me over the edge. I realize that I've been all wrapped up waiting for him to call so I could tell him about Spanky and Jessie and Samantha. And he doesn't even see it—that his taking off is a part of it—that we're all forced to feed on each other's misfortunes. It's like the teeth in Jessie's nightmare, coming out of thin air to gobble us whole. I let loose and howl like I haven't since I was a kid, since even before my Dad left.

"Mags?" I can barely hear him over the racket I'm causing. I don't even care that everyone I never wanted to see me like this is staring aghast at me like I've just given everyone the third miracle. "Hey, Mags, don't cry. I'm coming over."

"What?" I sniffle. That's certainly enough to catch my attention. "What do you mean. Where are you?"

"I'm at my mom's. I came over to talk to her. And thank God, too. If this was long distance I'd totally have hung up on you."

I ignore that for more important details. "They talked to you? They let you in?"

"Yeah well, my mom let me in. She finally kicked the old man out. She's been waiting to hear from me. Her boyfriend was there. Aagh," he makes this choking sound. I can tell he's got a finger poised inside his mouth—the classic barforama sign. "So I'll be over soon, alright?"

I tell myself I don't care when the phone goes dead and I shuffle back into my room. I tell myself, it doesn't matter whether he comes over. He wasn't here and I needed him. And I'm crying because all those people in the kitchen have all shrunk in my head. Not that they've turned into the Little People or anything—but they're smaller. Nat, Benny. Hell, even Spanky. They've turned into people I don't necessarily admire all that much, people I can't put any faith in. So I'm still crying, keening like a goddamn banshee, when he knocks on my bedroom door an hour later and carries in two plates of sandwiches and tea.

He's tanned, healthier than I've ever seen him. Bronze all over, almost the almond hue that reminds me of his mother's skin. He takes my hand, shoves a plate in it, gives me an awkward half-hug. We're quiet for a few minutes. PK pushes his glasses up his nose and shoos away hair that's fallen over his face. It's like I'm looking at a new person. I recognize the gestures but he's not the same PK. It's almost as if, in the weeks of his departure, he's grown years instead of a couple months. He's filled out more. His chest isn't as scrawny as it was. As if he's grown up and left me behind in all this madness. Like he's seen outside the box.

"What's the boyfriend like?" I finally say, wanting to be polite.

"Typical asshole. My mom had a black eye. Says she walked into the cupboard."

It's kind of shocking, the way he says it. He doesn't even seem upset. His eyes, the eyes that used to make me think of words like 'summer' have gone chilly. And I'm thinking, where the hell did PK go? When did this happen? All I can do is stare at him, search for a glimpse of my old PK, the one who belongs only to me. The one who's got a heart bigger than Atlantic Canada. There's a hot lump behind my eyes, and one gigantic one permanently residing in my throat. I try to gulp it down long enough to say, "You didn't say goodbye."

"I'm sorry," he says. He doesn't sound sorry.

"How could you do that to me? I was so fucking worried about you. Spanky and me. Fuck. We went all over town looking for you. I called the goddamn hospitals. I called the fucking morgue, Peek. What—almost two months and you couldn't even pick up the goddamn phone?"

He's filling his lungs, lighting a cigarette. I pinch it and he lights another. It hits me then the difference—it's not just that he's not so skinny or anything. He's less fragile, as though for once he could stand up against the bullshit all on his own. But it's also like he's let go of something beautiful, that special thing that made me love him more than anything.

"I didn't do it to hurt you," he starts.

"You could have called collect. Fran wouldn't have cared."

"I wasn't even aware of what I was doing at first, eh? I'd walked down to the bridge off the strip down by the water, where it turns into the highway, right? You know how it gets all stopped up in the afternoon and clogged with traffic. So all these cars were just sitting there and I was walking so I just—stuck out my thumb. All these voices had been going around and around in my head, and they were getting all tangled up." He pulls his hand out and stares at it, as if it was steeped with magical powers beyond his own understanding. "This truck stopped. I got in. I think—" he pauses, looking thoughtfully at the map on my wall, "I think I was trying to get some perspective." He puts his musing face on while he sucks at his cigarette.

"You were supposed to take me with you, you prick."

"It's not something I planned or anything. Everything was closing in, y'know? I needed to know what it was like, to see if I really could escape. I needed to know that my life wasn't over before it had begun." He shrugs and starts looking for my ashtray. "But there's something else."

"What now."

"This might hurt you, Mags, but just hear me out."

"Isn't that what I'm doing? Aren't I being polite enough for you?"

"Yeah. Well. I didn't think you'd come."

"Excuse me?"

"I mean, I thought you were just going to talk about it, and I'd be sitting here, twiddling my thumbs forever and feeling like I was dying a slow and painful death. I couldn't wait any longer. I had to see what the long distance runner was about, Mags, with or without you. I mean, you're so wrapped up in all of this," he spreads his hand as though my room and all outside it is pressing in on him. "You still believe in it. All of this. The Club."

"Fuck you, Pekoria."

"It's true though, isn't it? If you stopped and thought about it long enough."

I can't even respond to that. I'd rather knock his frigging head off. I'd like to punch him and say in a really tough voice, 'you have no idea, buddy.' I say instead, because after all, what's the point, "So now you know. What it's like."

"So now I know. And you know what else I found out, Mags?"

"What," I ask, and blow my nose.

"It's not the same all over. It's so much bigger. Maybe I wasn't seeing everything, but there's more out there than what's in here. There're some really nice people out there who will take stranger freaks in and treat them pretty decent."

I was twelve when PK and I fished my map out of the dumpster and nailed it carefully into the wall. I stare at it, stare holes through it, and I'm thinking to myself, you're so full of shit, Pekoria. You're just as full of it as the rest of them are. I sigh and say, "Peek, you forget so quickly."

The thing is, he's right. I probably wouldn't have gone, but not for the reasons he thinks. Maybe my former life as a cardboard box princess has taught me a thing or two. There's a trick to boxes. The thing is, boxes have four sides and PK's only seen out of one end. But there are other ends, real ends where the light spills out. And unless you've looked from every side you're never really out. And to do that you've at least got to have yourself intact. You've got to still care. And it's like a gigantic kick to the head to realize that my best friend, my smartest friend, isn't going to get out either. He can't. PK's never made a go at making the here and now better. He hasn't sat down and faced all the sides yet—he probably never will. And he's going to keep running until he does.

Just thinking this exhausts me all over again. "I want to sleep now," I tell him. "Go visit my brothers. They're having a party out there." I smash the cigarette out and I'm curling up again, not touching the food.

"Wait. About Spanky—"

"Go ask them." I nod to the door. "I don't wanna talk right now."

"They're organizing a wake—"

"Bully for them," I say.

"It's Saturday at the Club."

"Yeah and I'm going to sleep now. Do I look like I even know what day it is?"

"Sure. Sure, Mags. Listen, I'll be here when you get up, 'kay?" He soothes back my hair, tucks me in.

And I have to say it. It's in my throat, stuck and just waiting to come out. And I feel like my mother when I say it, old and tired beyond my years, "A very special anniversary, PK. It happened on her birthday. Same day as Samantha, same day as everything. Eerie, isn't it?"

His eyes go wide before they clamp down and shut it out.

I can tell it's sort of hit him deep. But he understands, now, what I'm all about. I've seen things, too.

And then I go, "Y'know, Peek, you were right about one thing."

"What's that, Mags," he says.

"We've gotta look at the possibilities of things. We may not be original," I say and sweep my hand across his cheek. "But we've gotta try to be." And then I decide I'm going to smoke again and I motion my hand for Peek to give me a cigarette. I light up and wrack my brain for another way to put things into perspective when I remember his drunken cafe rant. "You know what the real difference is? Between them and us, I mean." PK stares like suddenly he doesn't recognize me, either. "It's that when we start to see the world—and I mean really see it—it loses all fucking hope. And if there's one thing I've learned, PK, it's that people don't survive without that one ingredient."

This is all I've got to give him. I can't tell him about anything else—like meeting up with Jessie or what happened with Benny—because that means I'll have to tell him about himself in a less than flattering way. Hell, he probably wouldn't listen to me anyhow.

But even though everything feels upside-down and inside-out, I feel better. Lighter, somehow. It hurts like hell but I can feel myself letting go—letting go of the club, of the past, even of PK somehow. It's as if I'm looking up close and seeing something farther away, something that none of them can see yet. This is one girl who won't be climbing in front of a train or falling out of the sky. When I close my eyes again I'm not so scared of what I'll see—footprints in blood or people drowning in disaster.

Since PK's arrival I start to surface from my lair for tea, coffee and the occasional meal. Sometimes for a stiff whiskey.

Nobody seems to mind that I bum entire packs of cigarettes off them, that I haven't changed my clothes in days. It's a slow process, what I imagine coma victims face trying to reach sunlight when the nightmares claw them under and it's hard enough to breathe, let alone wake up.

There's a knock on my door. "Mags, want some tea?" This is Zach, who pokes his head in. The bedroom is dark, the blinds shut and fastened, blankets and pillows barricading out all avenues of light.

"Yeah," I croak. "I'll come out for it."

"Are you sure?"

"Yeah. Got any cigarettes? As if I've gotta ask."

"Mhhm," he nods. "Kettle's on. Got some soup on the stove, too. Mmm, your favourite."

"And what would that be, Bennett?"

"You know. That disgusting Lipton noodle stuff."

"Mhhm. Just feed me the cigarettes, Bennett."

"As you wish, Madam," he bows, making his exit.

The acid glasses I've been seeing the world through must be gone, because the kitchen has finally bent back into something I can recognize. The same degraded brown-patterned wallpaper, washed bare where cooking grease and smoke have taken root. The same plastic-covered chairs and plastic table. At the same time it all looks even smaller than I remember, as though I've suddenly grown eight inches and I'm seeing everything through the eyes of some giant. Zach's at the kitchen counter stirring tea. I take in the scene of these men, my brothers and Peek, sitting around the table. The knot that's been gnawing at me slips, turns sweet and sour all in the same gulp.

"Jesus H. on a bicycle riding backwards, Mags," Joe plucks up, "you sleep more than Rip Van."

"Would that be that speed metal band that rolled into

town last month?" I quip. Pete snorts into a cup and I'm suddenly glad not to be suffocating in the darkness anymore. It's sunny outside. There's a fuzzy light coming in through the windows, that summer light that seeps into the skin and eyes that makes me think of words like 'nostalgia'.

Pete pulls up a chair for me. Zach brings me a cup of tea just the way I like it, milky with loads of sugar.

"Uhm. What day is it today?"

"Friday," Peek goes.

"Oh. So tomorrow."

"Uh-huh."

"Joe," I go. "About Benny—"

Joe levels a look at me and I can tell he's not fobbing me off when he says, "Later." For a second I contemplate what it means, if he's figured it out. If Benny's confessed his sins and Joe's going to talk to Jackson about it. But that's a lot of 'ifs', and I'm not sure I really care too much at this moment.

So I just ask, "Promise?"

"Yup." Joe says. I get this shiver of revulsion when I realize just how seriously he's taking this. But it's going to be conducted *very* privately—Club rules.

"When was the last time you ate, Brat?" he asks, changing the subject. I shrug, turn to PK.

"You're still here."

His glasses bob in the light and I imagine they're floating upwards. I notice I'm lightheaded and there are these little fairy lights swimming all over the room. "Fran's been letting me crash until I can work things out with Mr. Sing. She's been real nice."

I pilfer a cigarette and wait for the news to crash over me before I respond. I still can't figure out why some of us are looked after and others aren't, but I also know I'll probably never figure it out. Everybody sort of looks away, embarrassed.

"Do you think you will?"

"Ahh, I dunno. Maybe?"

"What'll you do if you can't?"

PK gives me a crooked grin, "Kick my mother's boyfriend out?"

"Where the hell is Fran, anyways?"

Pete says, "Gone to the Mardi Gras office. After that she's job-hunting."

"Really," I go. "And what about you lugs?"

"What?" Pete looks concerned. "What'd you mean?"

"I mean, *brat*, why don't you guys get jobs, huh?"

"Shit, Mags, you feeling alright?"

"Peter Smith," I growl, "grow the fuck up."

Joe flashes a mouthful of teeth at me. "She's right, Pete. You're a fucking waste of space if I ever saw one."

"You're one to talk," I snort.

"No, because I'm actually going to be gainfully employed on top of my other activities."

"You're fucking joking." I can feel a grin spread across my lips, so much against my will. "Full-time?"

"Nah," Joe says, looking embarrassed.

"Doing what?" I ask. Joe shrugs and looks away.

"Doing what?" Pete echoes, his mouth hanging open.

"It's just a week's bouncing the Sphinx while Paul's on vacation. It's something, though."

"When the fuck did you have time to arrange that? Why didn't you fucking tell me?" Pete whines, looking all pissed.

"Because, asswipe, I wanted to get the job before I started lipping off about it. Unlike some people I know—"

"Drink your tea," Zach says over the bickering, pulling up a chair. "Then you gotta eat something. Fran made us swear we'd look after you while she's out."

I narrow my eyes, feel my tough self fill out my limbs after a long absence. "Chicken noodle, the Lipton's kind? And toast?"

He laughs. He looks relieved, at home. The way he hasn't been around me for quite a while. "Sure, Mags, whatever you say." Before I can think his arm comes around, squeezes my shoulder, and he kisses me on the lips.

I'm completely fazed. I look down at my t-shirt which is now completely wrinkled and filthy. "Hey," I say to Zach, "I think before I eat I might shower. Might even change my clothes." I turn back to PK. "Did your mom slip you any dough? We gotta dye our hair today, Peekster. Our roots are ugly."

"Speak for yourself," he says. He picks up a magazine, begins speedreading it. But I know he's home for now. This is how I know.

Acknowledgements

I owe a great debt to Patrick Carkin for sharing his archival materials of Samantha Smith with me. A special thank you to Mary di Michele, Rob Allen and Andre Furlani for their priceless insight and support. I would like to thank the writers of Mary di Michele's 1997 and Catherine Bush's 1998 prose workshops for their critical comments on this manuscript in its earliest stages.

Thanks to my writing comrades and friends Meg Sircom and Suki Lee for their unflagging encouragement and friendship, and reading the manuscript during its 'ugly phase', and Andy Brown for his excellent design work. Lilian Radovac also deserves praise for imbibing too much coffee with me, and spurring me on. And last but not least, thank you Peter Hewlett—for making me work harder, for your honesty, excellent advice and editing skills, being cute, and doing the dishes.

MEMBER OF SCABRINI MEDIA

Quebec, Canada
2002